A Case of Identity Theft

A CASE OF IDENTITY THEFT

A NEW SHERLOCK HOLMES MYSTERY

Craig Stephen Copland

Including the original Sherlock Holmes story -
A Case of Identity

Published by:
Conservative Growth
1101 30th Street NW
Washington, DC 20007

Cover design by Rita Toews.

ISBN: 1501095323
ISBN-13: 978-1501095320

DEDICATION

To Dr. James Alexander Copland, my older brother, whose paperback copy of Sherlock Holmes Stories I pinched and read and never forgot.

CONTENTS

ACKNOWLEDGMENTS

I discovered *The Adventures of Sherlock Holmes* while a student at Scarlett Heights Collegiate Institute in Toronto. My English teachers – Bill Stratton, Norm Oliver, and Margaret Tough – inspired me to read and write. Larry Scott, my Physical Education teacher, taught me the basics of rugby. I shall be forever grateful to them.

The plot of this novella is inspired by Arthur Conan Doyle's Sherlock Holmes Mystery *A Case of Identity.* Your enjoyment of this book will be enhanced by a quick re-read of that intriguing story. It is appended to this book.

My dearest and best friend, Mary Engelking, read all drafts, helped with whatever historical and geographical accuracy was required, and offered insightful recommendations for changes to the narrative structure, characters, and dialogue. Thank you.

Many words and whole phrases and sentences have been lifted and copied shamelessly and joyfully from the sacred canon of Sherlockian literature. Should any word or turn of phrase strike the reader as the *mot juste,* you may count on its having been plagiarized.

For the very idea of writing a new Sherlock Holmes mystery I thank the Bootmakers, the Sherlock Holmes Society of Toronto.

1 THE HAT

On one mid-November afternoon in the year 1888 Sherlock Holmes sat in his armchair, absently smoking on his pipe, and reading the weekend copies of London's newspapers. "Watson," he said, speaking my name but not looking up, "what is your opinion of this chap over there in America who claims he has discovered some sort of ray of light that can penetrate solid objects? He lacks sufficient imagination to even come up with a name for them, so they are being called 'X-rays?' You are a man of science, is there anything to them?"

"I believe that the chap you are reading about, Nicola Tesla, is a very clever fellow, but as far as there being a way for humans to see through walls, well, as they tell us up in Glasgow, I hae me doots."

"But just think," said Holmes. "If we could peer through the walls of all of these homes and buildings, would we not be in wonder at those things that are beyond the imagination that people, even Londoners, say and do to themselves and to each other when they are certain that they cannot be seen or heard by any outsider?

"It is precisely these tiny details of their lives that betray their motives and their machinations, and which I have trained myself to look for. Such a pity that all I am permitted to observe is what takes place outside of those impenetrable walls. If they ever do manage to make these wondrous new rays effective then you will find me standing on the pavements of London gazing into the most mundane of English houses."

"And," I countered with a chuckle, "about to be arrested by the local constable for being a Peeping Tom."

'Ah," said Holmes, still not looking up from the newspaper, "But I would be more than satisfied by restricting my observations to those who were fully clothed. Even to see and listen to them would solve a host of riddles and permit me to deduce answers to an endless list of unsolved crimes."

"If it is unsolved crimes you are seeking," I said, "why are you not devoting yourself to solving the one the Press has been screaming about for the past three months?"

"And what might that be?" said the voice from behind the newspaper.

"Really, Holmes," I protested. "You know perfectly well what it would be. I'm speaking of Jack the Ripper. Why has the nation's most accomplished detective not been involved in the case?"

Holmes uncharacteristically made no reply. This surprised me and I said nothing until a small light went on inside my head.

"Aha! You are involved in it. You are. I can tell."

"My dear friend," said the hidden voice, with just a small hint of impatience, "even to you, who I trust with my very life, I can say nothing. I will neither confirm nor deny any assertions you care to make. Although I would ask you to move on to other matters, as that case has been the subject of so much frenzied speculation that I am finding the entire matter tiring and tedious."

For a moment I said nothing, inwardly gloating. "Then you are involved. I knew it. But Mycroft must have recruited you and threatened to rap your knuckles if you ever let on to anybody. Admit it, old boy. I've got you on that one," I said triumphantly.

Holmes said nothing but he slowly lowered the newspaper, looked at me with just the barest hint of a smile, and then lifted it once again. "My good doctor," came the voice. "Do try your best to indulge me and stop commenting on the matter."

I ignored this request. "Well then, would the greatest detective mind in the Empire then offer his enlightened opinion on the matter? What is your scientific analysis of Mr. Jack the Ripper?"

"He does not exist."

"Nonsense Holmes. Five women have been murdered in the same manner and near the same location. How can you say the killer does not exist?"

"I did not say, my dear Watson, that there is no killer. I only said that Jack the Ripper does not exist."

"But of course he does," I protested. "He has sent taunting letters to the newspaper, *The Star*. He is daring the police to find him."

"The letters are a complete fabrication," replied Holmes.

"Oh really Holmes? Who would be so twisted and indecent as to impersonate a demented murdered and send a letter to the newspaper?"

"The newspaper."

"Yes, the newspaper. Did you not see it? You must have."

Holmes still had not looked directly at me. "My good man, you asked me a question and I answered it."

"I beg your pardon? Oh, so you are saying that the newspaper itself wrote a letter to itself? That's preposterous. The Press may be obnoxious and ill-mannered, but you cannot possibly be saying that they would entirely fabricate something and use it to deceive their readers?"

With this Holmes lowered the newspaper and looked steadfastly at me.

Readers of my stories recounting the adventures of Sherlock Holmes will recall that I have stated that, from time, to time something I have said has been responded to with The Look. In its mildest form, one of kindly but supercilious condescension, it says to me, without a word being uttered, that I am behaving like a naïve schoolboy. In mid-range it accuses me of being a pathetic dupe. The more severe variety, the third degree, announces that I am revealing to all that I am no more than an imbecilic moron. To my relief my question occasioned only the first degree.

"Very well then Holmes. The Press cannot be trusted in every single instance, but what purpose would they have in forging a letter and making up a clever name for a perverted murderer?"

"I would have thought that the answer was obvious. The *London Star* is a fairly new venture, needs to increase its circulation, thereby improving its profits and enriching its owners. Had the real murderer not come along they might have invented him if it were not for their utter lack of imagination. To them he was not sent "from Hell" but was as close to a godsend as could be hoped for. I imagine they even thanked the good Lord for sending him their way."

"My dear chap," I rebuked him. "You really are crossing the border from cynicism to blasphemy with that one. It is no doubt a good thing that you are not officially involved or Mr. Ripper might now be knocking on our door instead of the much less interesting one who is about to," I said, looking out of our window down to the pavement of Baker Street.

On that note Holmes finally put down the newspaper and stood and joined me at the window.

Wandering back and forth in front of the door to 221B Baker Street was what I concluded must have been a woman. My bewilderment resulted from my being unable to see anything except the top of a preposterously large hat. It not only obscured the bearer's head and shoulders but also the entire body, including the feet. All that could be seen from our vantage point was the top of the hat.

The hat approached our door, stayed there for a few seconds and then rotated counter-clockwise and bobbed several yards in the direction of Oxford Street. Then it stopped, rotated clockwise one hundred and eighty degrees, and returned to the door. Then another ninety degrees clockwise and flopped its way towards Marleybone before a final ninety degrees counter-clockwise and returning to our door and ringing the bell.

"Spare us," said Holmes. "Yet another young woman who is in love and confused. Were she a victim of a crime or a breach of promise she would have marched resolutely to the door, but being in love with the object of your quest renders the brain paralyzed and incapable of clear and logical deduction. Yet another reason, Watson, why I have found it best to avoid such disastrous entanglements."

"Mrs. Mary Angel," said Billy, the young page that Mrs. Hudson had recently hired to assist her in dealing with the endless stream of odd persons who crossed our threshold.

"How divine," I replied in response and congratulated myself on my outburst of quick wit by chuckling. Holmes did not even smile and I was left on my own to marvel at my droll humor.

The hat appeared behind Billy. As the hat was of short stature and Billy somewhat tall for his age, his body and head obscured the rest of the client, and all either Holmes or I could see was the massive hat flopping on the top of the page's pill box like a great set of wings.

"Please enter and be seated," said Holmes to the hat that having been circumnavigated by a backward-leaning page boy had now become a young woman in her early twenties. She sat and removed her hat, placing it in her lap.

"And," Holmes continued, "welcome back to London from your time in New Zealand and Australia, where you enjoyed writing stories about the tour of our English Footballers rugby team."

"Yes, Mrs. Angel," I added. "I quite enjoyed reading all about the triumphs of our boys out there in the Antipodes."

"Why thank you," replied the young woman as she seated herself on our sofa. "I had not expected that as a professional detective you would enjoy reading *Rugby Union News*."

In truth Sherlock Holmes not only did not enjoy reading this publication, he never read it at all, and never would. He had formed his conclusions, I was sure, by his observation of the lady's appearance and clothing and was, I was sure, mildly disappointed by the lack of any surprise from the would-be client.

I, on the other hand, as a sportsman who occasionally indulged in a small wager on the outcome of matches of all sorts, was a regular reader of the sporting newspaper that Mrs. Angel worked for, and had seen her byline attached to the reports of the recent tour of a British national rugby team to New Zealand and Australia.

"Indeed," I responded cheerfully, "it was a delight to read that our boys consistently trounced those upstarts in the colonies. Although you must have gotten a little weary writing the same thing every time. Twenty-two matches to just one for the local chaps, was it not?"

"Oh yes," she replied, looking at ease and smiling back at me. "It was quite the splendid time for our team as well as for my husband and me. We saw every match and journeyed up and down …"

"And he," interjected Holmes brusquely, not at all interested in letting any discussion of sporting events become the topic of conversation, "is, I gather, the reason for your being her today."

The smile vanished from her face and was replaced with a look of pained concern.

"Yes, sir," she answered. "He is. He has vanished." She brought her hands together as she spoke in an effort to stop the shaking that had begun in them. I could also see that she was biting on her lower lip to control the trembling that had set in.

"The facts, please madam," said Holmes. "When and where did you last see him? What communication have you had from him? What makes you sure that he is missing? And having told me all those matters do not forget to tell me his name, occupation, and family connections."

Mrs. Angel closed her eyes briefly and took a deep breath. "Of course sir. I will try my best to tell you everything I can. If it can help you to find him I would be most grateful."

"I make no promises, madam. I have not yet agreed to take on this case, if indeed it amounts to a case at all. Please get on with it."

2 ON A WILD GOOSE CHASE

Holmes lack of manners and consideration for young women in distress constantly vexed me, but I had learned over the years of watching him that he had a very soft place in his well-protected heart for the fairer sex, especially those who had been wronged and damaged by the men to whom they had given their trust. I could have told Mrs. Angel at that moment to relax and that Sherlock Holmes would ride to her rescue, but doing so would have angered England's finest detective beyond what I was willing to endure on an otherwise pleasant morning.

"My maiden name was Mary Sutherland. I grew up in the village of Coldfield, just outside Birmingham, as did my husband, Mr. Hosmer Angel. Our families were close friends and we, that is my husband and I, have been companions since we were children, and we were betrothed to each other, we liked to think, since we were ten years old. For the past several years we yearned to get married but our mothers, both of our fathers had passed away while we were children, but I do have a stepfather, insisted that we should be established and earning at least a modest income before doing so. That was a sensible thing to do and so we waited until we had both turned twenty-one, had secured gainful employment and had some prospects in front of us, and then were married following Michaelmas last year. Our first anniversary has just passed."

At this point tears began to appear in her eyes and her lower lip started to tremble. I leaned towards her and offered her the use of a clean handkerchief. Holmes did not move.

"Take another deep breath and keep going," he said. "Was your marriage pleasant or did the two of you make each other miserable?"

"Oh sir," she sputtered, "we could not have been happier. We had found very nice lodgings in Camberwell. Hosmer, my husband that is, had secured employment at Thomas Cook's Travel Service, and I, being a skilled typist, had set up a business offering typing to many of our local shop owners. I charged the going rate of twenty pence a page and was bringing in a steady income. Indeed I could scarcely handle any more. We were setting money aside, sensibly you know, and planned that in a year's time we would be able to start a family." Here she stopped and took another deep breath.

"Our only indulgence was that once a week, on the weekend, during the season, we would go and take our place in the stands and watch the Rugby Union matches. We never missed one when our home boys, Birmingham and Solihull, were playing and we could cheer them on. After the match we would treat ourselves to a pleasant supper down at Denmark Hill. We had a simple life, sir, but we could not have been happier."

"Of course. So what happened?" asked Holmes.

"You will recall sir, you being a fan of rugby union and all, that last winter it was announced that a national rugby union team would take a tour of New Zealand and Australia."

Holmes said nothing as he had no use for any such recollection. I responded pleasantly instead. "Of course, that was all through the sporting news. Quite the exciting opportunity for our boys, and for their loyal fans."

"Indeed it was sir," she returned with a look that was not quite a smile but at least she was no longer crying. "Cook's had been given the contract to make all the bookings and because Hosmer, my husband that is, was such a rugby fan, and of course because he was a diligent clerk, he was given the assignment of being the guide and managing the tour. He was quite over the moon about it but would not agree to do so unless I could accompany him. Well then, the managers at Cook's sent a word over to the *Rugby Union News* and then sent me to speak to them, and as I was a strong typist and had some skills as a story-teller, they hired me to be their reporter for the tour."

"And congratulations on getting the job and sending back such fine reports," I said with unfeigned enthusiasm.

"Oh, thank you sir, but I must admit that much of the reason was that the newspaper would be able to claim that they had a reporter on the spot and have their stories sent back, but it would cost them a pittance as my travel and lodgings were already paid for by the team tour. But it was unusual to have a young woman report on rugby sir. Some of the older chaps were quite jealous. I would like to think that the editors were enlightened and supporters of universal suffrage, but I have to confess that they were merely pinching their pennies."

"Keep going," said Holmes. He gave me a bit of a look that said that I was becoming a distraction. However, as all loyal fans of rugby union know, there are some things that cannot be avoided and have to be endured.

"Of course, sir," she said. "The tour was like the honeymoon that folks in our station in life can only dream about. The ocean journey on the Steamship Kaikoura was glorious even if the cabin we were assigned was not what you could call posh. But the food and the music – the rugby boys are great singers you know. Welsh many of them. Some of the songs were a little rude but that's just the way they are, especially after a few rounds of ale. We laughed and danced all the way to the far side of the world and back. And the matches were glorious. We won all but one, as you have noted doctor. But there was nothing at stake except the fun of the game. The Kiwis, as the New Zealanders like to call themselves, were wonderfully hospitable, and even if we beat them on the field they always joined us afterwards in the pubs.

"Their players brought along their wives and girlfriends, who were very nice and refined young women. We in England do them a great disservice by lumping them in with the Australians, you know. The New Zealanders are really much more, well, civilized I guess you could say. And since many of our boys are still bachelors we were joined by a number of quite attractive young ladies in search of a sturdy young gentleman who had good prospects as a husband. Rugby players are not well-known for acting like gentlemen of course, sir, but most of our lads came from good families. Two young women did manage to land a couple of our lads, and they were married by the ship's captain and returned to England with us. And all in all the tour was just a great success and we, my husband and I that is, could not have been happier."

"And then when you returned to England he disappeared?" said Holmes.

"No. Well, yes, but not immediately," she replied. "When we arrived back in London I had to return to our lodgings in Camberwell and work very hard to get my business back, as I had neglected it for five months. But Hosmer was called immediately to Cardiff. The Welsh national team had observed the success of our tour and wanted one of their own next year. Cook's sent my husband to meet with them and he was not only to be the tour guide but he had been selected to manage all the negotiations and business arrangements. It was quite the feather in his cap. So we were apart from each other for over a week. But we were both so busy that we hardly had time to miss each other. And then . . ." Here she paused.

"Yes?" said Holmes.

"And then this letter arrived in the post." She reached into her purse and produced an envelope and handed it to Holmes. He read it and handed it to me. It was typed on plain paper and ran:

My dearest:

Unbelievably good news! We are to return to New Zealand at once. The Kiwis are sending a rugby team made up entirely of natives to England. It will be a sport and exotic culture tour combined. Cook's has the travel contract and I have been chosen to manage it. My salary has been doubled. I said I could not go unless you came as well and they had already spoken to the *News*, who were so pleased with your work, and made that arrangement. I cannot believe our good fortune.

My dearest, we must make arrangements very quickly. The next steamer for the Antipodes departs on October the twenty-forth, just three days from now my dearest. I will have to meet you on board. Please, dearest, re-pack and get ready to go. Your ticket is enclosed. I shall not need to pack as I have enough with me already. I will board at the last minute and then will be fully engaged with meetings until dinner. But I will see you for dinner and dancing at our table at six o'clock after our ship is out to sea.

My dearest, how could we be luckier? Another honeymoon! See you on board.

Your happy husband,

Hosmer

Enclosed with the letter were the stubs and receipts from Mrs. Angel's ticket.

"I was in ecstasy," the young woman said quietly. "It seemed that my life had been transformed into a fairy tale. I did not sleep for the next two days what with laundry and packing. I took a cab to the Union pier and boarded the Oceana two days later. Our cabin was two decks higher than the last trip and the help very accommodating. I imagined myself lifted into the noble classes. I enjoyed walking the promenade as we pulled away from the shore and bade good bye to England. Just before six o'clock I dressed and made my way to the dining room and took my place at our table, and it was such a good table, and I waited."

Here she again paused. "I waited, and he did not arrive at the table. At first I thought nothing of it and assumed that his meetings had run overtime. But he did not show up that evening and at ten o'clock I went searching for him. I asked about meetings being held and no one on the crew knew anything about any such meetings. I waited in the cabin. I was awake all night long. He did not arrive. First thing in the morning I asked to speak to the captain and at noon had an appointment with him. He said he was sorry for everything that had happened to me, but he checked the list of passengers and although my name was listed my husband's was not. He was quite kindly but he clearly saw in me an abandoned wife who had been deceived by a wayward husband. I gathered that it happens often on such journeys."

"You were not the first, I regret to inform you, Mrs. Angel, and you will not be the last," said Holmes.

"Sir," she pleaded. "You must not believe that I was abandoned. Hosmer would not do that to me. I have known him since we were children. I know his heart. He has a good heart. He would never do anything to hurt me so terribly. Something dreadful has happened to him. I know it has. You have to help me. You have to help me find him."

"First things first," said Holmes. "Please continue your story."

"Yes, of course, sir," she said. "By this time we had rounded Gibraltar and were into the Mediterranean. There was a stop scheduled for Marseille the next day and I got off the ship there. What little money I had with me I used to have my baggage transported to a small hotel near the docklands where I found cheap lodgings. A woman alone was not at all safe and I was fearful of walking on my own. However, I said a prayer and made my way to the nearest British bank and arranged to have funds transferred from our saving account in London.

"The money arrived two days later. With that I purchased train fare back to Calais and booked passage across the Channel and home. A week had passed since I had boarded the Oceana. I contacted my mother in the Midlands and she immediately called her friend, Hosmer's mother, Mrs. Angel, Mrs. Angel senior that is, as I am now also Mrs. Angel. She was very disturbed as Hosmer had sent her word that he was meeting me on the ship and we were returning to New Zealand."

"Ah," said Holmes. "That is material. Your husband had also sent word that he intended to travel with you?"

"Yes sir, and he does not lie. He does not lie to me and he would never lie to his mother. Even if he ever wanted to he never could lie to his mom. So he must have been telling the truth when he said he was to meet me on the ship and sail to New Zealand."

"Hmm," said Holmes. His telltale sign was giving him away. He had placed his hands in front of his body, his fingertips touching each other. He was staring quite intensely at Mrs. Angel.

"Please, miss. Do continue," he said.

"There was no sign of his having been in our rooms recently. So I contacted his employer, Thomas Cook's travel. They were very courteous as all travel service providers are, but they informed me that Hosmer had completed his assignment in Cardiff and had given his notice, all very rushed and all, because he was leaving for New Zealand because of the position I had been offered by *Rugby Union News.* They had wished him well and told him to try and secure the travel contract to bring the native rugby players to England, as they thought it might be awarded to a local firm in Auckland. But they had given him no assignment and were quite firm in saying that they had not issued tickets, good tickets they were, for my husband and I to travel half around the world and back."

"Your story has a certain symmetry to it," said Holmes, now with his eyes closed. "Quite interesting."

"Then sir, I went to speak to the good men at *Rugby Union News.* They had been very nice to me, even if they had been penny pinchers. I told them my story, including the parts about talking to the people at Thomas Cook's. They were quite sympathetic, they rather liked me a little I like to think, but they floored me when they said that no offer of any sort had been made to me, and that they had never spoken to the people at Thomas Cook's, and that they had no plans to sponsor any part of the native Maori rugby team for they were of the belief that rugby should only be played by gentlemen, and only then by amateurs, and that there had been rumors that some of the New Zealand natives were receiving cash secretly to come and play in England and they would not be part of any such arrangement. No sir.

"I was utterly shamed in front of them but they were still courteous to me and one of the older chaps – I wouldn't have expected it of him since he was one of the old boys who had objected to my being given the assignment with our national team – he took me aside and asked me a few more question, in private like and all. He said he would help me because he had read my stories and thought they were so good that no one could have known they were written by a woman had my name not been attached to them; and he thought I was a right good rugby fan, for a woman that is, and that I knew the game quite well, for a woman of course, and had a right good passion for it in my soul, at least as much could ever hope for from a woman. So he gave me your name and address, Mr. Holmes, and sent me to see you straightaway, and he even offered to loan me the money to pay your fee if I needed it, which was very good of him as he is far from wealthy himself, and I thought that was about as kind and generous as I could ever hope to expect, from a man that is."

"And now you are here," said Holmes. "Remind me please Watson to send a note of thanks to the right good gentleman at the *News.*"

"Indeed I shall," I said. "Right good of him was it not?"

"Now madam," said Holmes. "About this letter you received from your husband. Was he in the habit of writing letters to you?"

"Oh yes sir. He and I wrote to each other since we were ten years old whenever we could not see each other for more than three days. He always wrote such wonderful letters sir. They were always full of affection and sometimes even a bit naughty, if you know what I mean sir, but I believe that it is not a bad thing between a husband and wife is it sir?"

Holmes wisely did not attempt an answer to the question but carried on with questions of his own.

"This letter has been typed. Was your husband a typist?"

"Oh no sir. I wouldn't let him near my typewriter sir. He was all thumbs as they say. But I thought that with him being promoted to a manager level almost at Thomas Cook's that he must have been given a secretary to help him, which made me quite proud of him and all. So I thought it most unusual to receive a letter like that but I made sense of it and then thought nothing of it."

"He addressed you as 'dearest', twice I believe," said Holmes. "Was that his usual term of endearment for you? If not, what did he call you? Please just be frank in your answer. Doctor Watson and I observe the strictest confidence with all clients."

I thought of adding 'and especially with young women having troubles in their love lives' but I refrained.

"No sir," said Mrs. Angel. Then she looked at the floor and I could see a blush rising into her face. For a moment she said nothing, and then shrugged her shoulders and spoke. "He always called me his heaven-sent little heifer, and I called him my bully-boy. We were raised in a farming village, sir, and I will have to let you take things from there and please do not ask me to say more on that sir."

Here I spoke up for fear, knowing Holmes, that he was quite likely to do the opposite of what she had just asked. "Mrs. Angel, you may be sure that we understand and will not pursue that line any farther. And may I, as a doctor, tell you that you are a fortunate young woman to have some a warm and playful relationship with your young husband."

She looked up, still blushing. "Thank you doctor. You are being very considerate."

"Fortunately I am not the same way inclined," said Holmes, "or I would never get to the end of my questions. So just one last item with regards to your letter. He was not only uncharacteristically discreet but he did not even sign his name to it. Had that ever happened before?"

"No sir, but as I said sir, I assumed that he must have dictated it to a secretary and therefore he had to be very proper and all, and that the secretary had just typed his name because that is what secretaries do when they are in a hurry, or at least that is what I concluded must have happened, sir."

Holmes said nothing in response. He closed his eyes and folded his long legs under his body, brought his hands together, fingertips pointing up, and held that pose for a full two minutes. Mrs. Angel stared at him and then looked at me with bewilderment all over her face. I reached out my hand and laid it on her forearm, then lifted it in a silent gesture that told her to just wait. She must have thought Sherlock Holmes a very queer bird indeed, but he returned from his imaginary flight to who-knows-where and spoke.

"I will accept this case, madam. I cannot promise anything except that you will have my utmost effort and my complete confidence. Kindly leave your card behind and we will be in contact with you as soon as we have anything to report. In the meantime I suggest that you resume your typing business as it may be financially necessary as well as distracting. And may I wish you good day, Mrs. Angel." With this he unfolded his legs, rose and gestured towards the door. The young woman rose, the look of bewilderment still somewhat on her face, and made to exit.

"Thank you Mr. Holmes, and thank you doctor," she said as she replaced her monstrous hat on her head and walked down the stairs. I watched from the window as she stood on the pavement on Baker Street, but I quickly jumped back when she turned and looked up.

Fortunately her line of sight was blocked by the hat. When I looked back down I saw the hat climb into a cab.

"Very well then Holmes," I began. "Even if your newest client was not surprised at what you knew about her I was, so do tell how you deduced all you did. I am sure you are itching to tell me. You always are."

He looked a little miffed as he took his scientific observations and deductions quite seriously, but he deigned to enlighten me all the same.

"Her finger nails were clipped short rather than being allowed to grow to a fashionable length, and the fleece on the cuffs of her sleeves has two parallel lines marked on them. Together a sure sign of a typist. Her face was sunburned sometime in the past three weeks as could be seen by the faint peeling still on her forehead. As there is no sunshine capable of giving a sunburn anywhere in the British Isles she must have been abroad to someplace much warmer and only recently returned; obviously an ocean voyage to the tropics. Her boots and her dress were quite new and of good quality but two years out of style indicating that she had bought them in one of the colonies where our merchants send all of their fashions after they have gone out of style here, as the colonists do not know any better and rush to buy them. Why would an earnest young typist be returning from a warm colony at this time of year? It is not reasonable to think she would have gone there to seek employment? The colonies are chock full of cheap labor. Therefore she must have been sent, and who would send a typist on an ocean voyage other than a newspaper? And what newspaper could possibly have sent someone in the recent past except for that miserable little *Rugby News,* of which I am most certainly not a reader, but the news of the tour was mentioned in *The Times.* As to her being worried about her husband the obvious clue was the wedding ring. I could see that her finger was red and swollen on both sides of the ring – an obvious indication that she had been grasping and twisting it quite desperately, as do so many women who are distraught concerning their wayward husbands. All put together it was more than enough to come to the conclusions I did."

"Remarkable as always, Holmes," said I. "Of course I knew all that, except the husband part, as soon as Billy gave the name since I do read the *Rugby Union News* and had read all of her stories. Quite a good way to keep up on what is happening, you know. I might recommend it to your reading list."

Holmes harrumphed, sat down, and lit his pipe.

"What I do not understand," I said, "is why you accepted this case. You normally do not give those with affairs of the heart the time of day. Why this one?"

"Aha, because this is not a case of a lovesick wife and a wandering husband. There is something behind this, Watson. A return ticket to Auckland, 'and a good ticket it was'. Someone has invested at least a hundred pounds to get her out of the country. The letter is not from her husband but some other party. From what little we know the husband may have been similarly deceived. There is no hint of another romantic interest, and no longstanding passions or hatreds. So the only other motive must be financial gain. And it must be significant for someone to have made such an extensive and expensive plan to get the poor thing out of the way."

"And you are quite sure," I returned, "that the young husband could not have had another love interest. It does happen you know. Especially amongst the young athletic crowd."

"Quite right you are. I thought that at first, when I looked at her, did you not? What did you make of her?"

"Well," I said. "She is no beauty that would turn heads in Trafalgar Square, but she seems pleasant enough."

"Oh my dear doctor. You are entirely too kind. She was not the least bit attractive. Her face was vacuous if not bovine. Of late we have been quite fortunate to have been blessed with clients from such splendid places as Goa, or Trinidad where the mongrel races are loveliest on earth. Even the Scots and Irish lasses who have come through our door have been more than comely. We forget that we English are a singularly unattractive race. I had fully expected that Mr. Hosmer Angel had been bewitched by some Maori maiden but her confession of their terms of endearment disabused me of that notion. Any young husband who joyfully takes his wife to rugby union games, and refers to her as his . . . what inane thing did he call her? 'My heaven-sent little heifer' – good lord what romantic notions will do to addle the brain – is quite obviously besotted with affection. That, sir, was what led me to conclude that there was a mystery to be solved, robbery of some sort to bring to justice, and quite likely foul play to be avoided. It has the promise of a fascinating case. Would you not agree, Watson?"

"If you say so, Holmes," I nodded in agreement, although not altogether comfortable with his inconsiderate observations about the English race.

3 THE WAYWARD HUSBAND

I saw little of Sherlock Holmes for the next three days. He came in late in the evening, caught three or four hours sleep at most, and then departed at first light in the morning. On Thursday in the late afternoon he appeared looking tired but smiling.

"You have solved your case," I exulted. "Well done. Are we to celebrate?"

"Ah, not quite so quick to the final conclusion, my dear Watson. A part of it has been solved. The young husband has been at least located and is, I fully expect, on his way back to his forlorn young wife. That is all good. The mystery behind what took place still remains, and I am still in a fog about it. But I can do no more sleuthing about this evening so I suggest dinner. Marcini's?"

"Delighted to join you. Let me alert Mrs. Hudson that she need not prepare anything for us."

Over an excellent Italian dinner and a generous decanter of Chianti Holmes explained his progress to date.

"My real interest in this case is the mystery behind it. However, I have to discipline myself and put first things first. My priority must always be the safety and well-being of my client, and that meant that before doing anything else I had to locate and return to Mrs. Angel, her husband. It took some basic detective work but I visited every steamship company's office and asked to review their recent passenger lists. It is fortunate that they keep such records, unlike the railroads. It makes finding lost husbands so much easier.

"They are however rather protective of their passengers' privacy and not all that eager to reveal their lists, so it took some time to find a way to be able to review them in detail. I shan't explain how except to say that several disguises, even to the point of becoming a repellant masher and preying upon the foolishness of a young bookkeeper, were put to good use. I did discover that on the Cunard vessel, the S.S. Aurania, was a passenger named Hosmer Angel, and that it departed from the India Pier at half past six on the same date as the Union line's Oceana did."

"And to where was it destined," I asked, quite curious.

"Also to the Antipodes, with stops in both Sydney and Auckland. More than coincidence, is it not Watson?"

"Indeed it is."

"I then removed any disguise and asked to speak to the office manager. I told him who I was and that I had been retained by the wife of one of their passengers who was very concerned for her husband's safety. The young chap gave me an odd look and asked if I could come with him immediately to the office of their director of security. The director, a fellow I remembered from his having worked for Scotland Yard in the past. He sought greener and more lucrative pastures, or I suppose I should say 'waters' with Cunard. The chap sat me down and in a most serious voice told me a remarkable story that the captain of the Aurania had wired back from Cairo.

"He said that, yes indeed, Mr. Hosmer Angel had boarded at India pier on the twenty-fourth of October. Late in the evening, after the ship was well into the Channel, he came banging on the captain's door very distraught demanding that a search be started immediately for his wife, as he could not locate her. Well didn't the captain just order up a crew and they did a thorough search from stem to gudgeon and found nothing and feared she might have fallen overboard or some such awful fate. But one of the clerks thought to check the passenger manifest and reported to the captain that only Mister Angel's name was on the list, but not his wife.

"On showing this to Mr. Angel the poor man became extremely disturbed, in an outright panic. First he demanded that the ship be turned around and sailed back to London. The captain of course could not comply. And then he demanded that they let him off at the nearest port of call. Again the captain had to decline as they were not scheduled to call at any port before Alexandria. The captain, having commanded many passenger vessels, was not unfamiliar with distraught husbands or wives looking for their respective spouses and becoming highly disturbed. It took several days before they reached their first port and stopped there prior to entering the Suez. All the while this poor chap paced the decks and asked the other passengers repeatedly if they had seen his wife at the pier, or on the boat, or anywhere. As soon as the gangplank was lowered he scampered down, carrying what little baggage he had brought on board, and has not been heard from since.

"Now Cunard is a very respected line and they do not like it at all when passengers disappear, especially a few miles from Cairo where goodness only knows what could happen to them. The director chap asked me if I had heard anything and I informed him that while I had not I was reasonably sure that he could relax and the young Mr. Angel would find his way by hook or by crook back to London and would re-appear within a few more days. And that, my dear friend, is what I am quite confident will happen."

"Well now, I suppose that is some good news. Mrs. Mary Angel will be very relieved."

"And after making my report to her tomorrow after breakfast, I shall be able to turn my mind to whatever the very strange mystery is behind our travelers."

Two days later we were enjoying a fine English breakfast when there was a furious banging on our door. Young Billy answered it and all we heard next was his shouting, "Sir! Really sir! You cannot just charge in here, sir!" His shouts were accompanied by heavy footsteps as our newest visitor scaled the seventeen steps in a few bounds. He burst into our room, dropped his valise with a thud, and shouted at us, "Which of you is Sherlock Holmes?"

He was young and slender, with an athletic physique. His suit and his entire appearance were a complete mess. He had not shaved in several days, nor, it appeared, had he slept. His clothes were terribly disheveled and even in the cool of the early autumn morning he was sweating profusely and gasping for breath.

Holmes rose from our table. "Good morning Mr. Hosmer Angel, we have been expecting you, but forgive us, we were not expecting you quite so early. I am Sherlock Holmes and I hope that your journey by tramp steamer across the Mediterranean was not overly stressful. I gather the train from Milan was a little more comfortable. I assure you that your lovely wife is quite safe and before I direct you to her please tell me how it is that I find you at 221B Baker Street so early this morning?"

The poor Mr. Angel looked at Holmes as if he were the opposite of anything angelic. He spoke hesitantly.

"I do not know how you knew all these things. Yes, I took a tramp steamer from the port of Alexandria to Genoa. On the dock there a stranger met me and spoke in perfect English. He handed me a card with your name and address and a generous amount of cash with which I was able to purchase a train ticket, and told me to come directly to you as soon as I returned to London. I have no explanation for anything that has taken place in my life for the past ten days sir. Please tell me, where is my wife?"

"Of course, young man. Mrs. Angel is now waiting for you at Number 31 Lyon Place in Camberwell. I believe you are familiar with that address?"

"That is where I live sir. She is there and waiting for me? Are you sure?"

"Absolutely positive. So please be on your way post haste. Ah, but I have two requests. Please leave behind the letter you received from your wife telling you about her assignment and the departure time of the ship, and please be so kind that you and your good wife make an appointment to see me within the next two days. There are some matters that must be cleared up."

Hosmer Angel did not answer. He reached into the pocket of his suit and retrieved an envelope, somewhat the worse for wear and having been assaulted by several days' sweat. He handed it to Holmes all the while looking at him as if he were viewing an apparition. Then he picked up his valise and bounded back down the stairs. The last I saw of him he was running pell-mell down Baker Street and shouting at a cabbie.

"I would have preferred to have questioned him at length," said Holmes, "but breakfast is getting cold, and it is in the interest of my client that her husband return to her without delay. So we shall just have to wait for two days. Meanwhile, Watson, relax and enjoy your breakfast and I will do the same. After which I will resume my efforts to discern what is behind this most peculiar case."

"Not so quickly, Holmes," I protested. "How in the name of heaven did that poor fellow happen to run into somebody on the docks of Genoa who knew who he was, gave him your name, and sent him back to London? You were behind that, I am sure. But how did you do it?"

"Elementary, my dear Watson. It was a spot too far to send my Irregulars so I had to borrow some of Mycroft's."

"Mycroft, your brother? He has street urchins working for him in Europe? That's unimaginable!"

From my others stories about Sherlock Holmes the reader will remember that Mycroft Holmes did not merely work for the British Government, he *was* the British Government. His title was some non-descript assistant to some non-descript Secretary, but in his head he held the exact memory of everything that had taken place in Westminster, or Whitehall, or in every far-flung corner of the Empire for the past thirty years. He was the *eminence grise* behind every minister or prime minister. It mattered not which party was in power. He had memorized the dossier on every Member of Parliament of every party and knew far more about them that they could afford to have set free on the streets of London. He was paid well to know everything, to advise on all significant concerns, and to say nothing. He had agents everywhere.

"Not at all. Except he does not call them Irregulars. I believe that his usual word for them is 'spies.' He has a network all over the continent and he sent out the alert. He would never have acted had it only been a case of yet another philandering husband but when I told him the details and imparted my thoughts he simply said that this was not the first case he had heard about. Something similar and much nastier had taken place recently in Oslo. Beyond that he said no more but clearly he put his not insignificant network to work. We appear to be on to something, Watson. This endearing if not altogether attractive young couple are likely only pawns in a much wider web and I must address whatever faculties I have to understanding it, and, Lord willing, vanquishing it."

He said no more, but finished his breakfast in silence, then donned his hat and cape and left the room. I watched as he climbed into a cab and proceeded south towards Marble Arch.

4 THE MOTHERS

Two days passed and there was no return visit of Mr. and Mrs. Angel. I asked about them in passing and Holmes responded, "They had a rather traumatic experience and if they are like most your married couples, and I fear they are, they will take several days before re-engaging with the civilized world."

Then the third day passed and then the fourth. Holmes was showing some signs of concern.

"I sent them a note, late yesterday asking them to come and see me but I have heard nothing," he answered in response to my query. The tone of his voice told me that he was not feigning his worry as he was wont to do from time to time for theatrical effect and disguise.

Late on the fourth day we heard the bell on Baker Street. Billy appeared at our door shortly afterwards bearing a visitor's card. "A Mrs. Angel," he began but he got no further before Holmes interrupted.

"Show the young lady up right way," he said, restraining his obvious desire to shout at the lad.

"Begging you pardon, Mr. Holmes, sir," the boy replied with well-taught manners under duress. "There are in fact two ladies, and I have been taught never to say that a lady is old sir. But neither of these are what I could ever call young, sir."

Holmes glared at the poor lad. I responded, "Quite alright, there Billy. Do show up whoever it is that is waiting at our door and don't leave them out in the cold." Then I turned and beckoned for Mrs. Hudson. "Mrs. Hudson, we have some fine ladies of your vintage joining us. Would you mind awfully organizing a bit of tea?"

"Right, doctor. Be there soon," came the reply for our ever-indulgent landlady.

Coming up the stairs were two women of a certain age, old enough to have adult children but not yet old enough for a brood of grandchildren. They were not so much conversing as they climbed the stairs as nattering back and forth. I tried to listen for a complete sentence but heard none.

They entered our parlor. Both were dressed in sensible dark dresses and overcoats such as might be seen in the Midlands last winter or in London ten years ago. They were both about five foot two or three and wore sensible-looking flat shoes. Both had hair that had gone a little gray with shades of blonde left behind in the one and of a darker chestnut in the other.

The first one to come through the door advanced towards Sherlock Holmes and extended her hand. "Good morning, Mr. Holmes. I am Bedelia Windibank and this is my friend Mrs. Angel." Whereupon the second came forward extending her hand and said, "Good morning Mr. Holmes. I am Gertrude Angel and this is my dear friend Mrs. Windibank."

This little ritual was then repeated for my benefit. Holmes had been mannered enough to stand but said nothing. I acknowledged their greeting. “Honored to make your acquaintance, aren’t we Mr. Holmes. Please be seated and enjoy a cup of tea. I gather you have come some distance to London.”

Holmes said nothing and continued to stare at them.

“Oh yes, some distance,” said Mrs. Windibank.

“Yes quite a ways,” said Mrs. Angel.

The reader will forgive me if, for reasons that become obvious, I cease to give full attribution to what was said in the minutes that followed and use only abbreviations.

“We came down from just outside Birmingham last evening.” (Mrs. A)

“We started from Coldfield, a mile north of Birmingham, yes.” (Mrs. W)

“We are quite concerned about our children.” (A)

“Very worried we are about my daughter and Mrs. Angel’s son.” (W)

“We heard all about their very strange and trying escapade on the high seas.” (A)

“And then they told us about the way you helped them, Mr. Holmes.” (W)

“They both said quite emphatically that the famous detective, Sherlock Holmes, had aided them. Indeed that is what they said.” (A)

“That was three days ago.” (W)

“Going on four.” (A)

“You can imagine that we were greatly relived as we had not heard from either of them for over a week prior to that.” (W)

"That was the week when they were on their wild goose chase of each other in the steamships." (A)

At this point, dear reader, I lost track of who was saying what so forgive me if the attributions are dropped altogether. It will make no difference I assure you.

"So we made our way from Coldfield to London, and paid a visit to their lodgings."

"We paid a visit this afternoon. And what do think we found?"

"Nothing. Not a trace of them."

"They were gone."

"Completely."

"Vanished."

"Not a trace."

"You already said that."

"Indeed I did. I already said that."

At this point Sherlock Holmes interrupted. "My dear ladies. Are you telling me that your children, Mr. and Mrs. Angel, are missing."

"Only the younger Mrs. Angel. Mrs. Angel senior has not vanished."

"I am sitting right here. So obviously I have not vanished. Only Mrs. Angel Junior."

"That younger one."

"That's what I just said."

"Actually my dear, you said 'Junior' which is an appellation used by Americans, not the English."

"Ladies! Please! Where have your children gone?" shouted Holmes.

That shut up our visitors, but not for long.

"Mr. Holmes, that is why we are here."

"Why do you think we came to see you?"

"If we knew where they were we wouldn't need to ask you. We are trying to be sensible about this, you know sir."

"Why would we have come to England's most famous detective if we knew where they were? That would make no sense at all. You see we don't know where they are."

"They've vanished."

"Without a trace."

"They were supposed to come and see me two days ago." Holmes said rather more loudly than necessary. "Do you have any idea why they did not do so?"

"Oh yes. They told us that Uncle Peter had arrived in town."

"That's my daughter's Uncle Peter, not Mr. Angel's."

"But he calls him Uncle Peter as well, of course. Very dear to both families he is."

"He just arrived from New Zealand and sent for both of them."

"He wanted to see them right away. He's rather old and not in good health."

"Might not be with us much longer. So he wanted to see them immediately."

"He just arrived all the way from New Zealand."

"He's been there since he was a boy, he has. He's come all the way around the world to see the two of them."

"Said he had to see them now they were married."

"Pity he could not have come sooner and been at the wedding."

"Oh yes. It was a very pretty wedding. Pity he could not have been there."

"But he did get to see them, all the same. Sent me a note saying he was glad he did. But now they're gone missing."

"Vanished."

"Without a trace."

At this point I took pity upon Sherlock Holmes. I noticed Mrs. Hudson standing in the doorway trying very hard not to burst out in uncontrolled laughter. So I summoned her to my side.

"My dear Mrs. Hudson, could you perhaps bring these ladies another cup of tea. I do believe they have run dry."

"Of course I will doctor. And ladies you will have to enjoy it quickly before it gets cold. Nothing to ruin the taste of good tea like letting it get cold you know."

With this she filled up their cups and they devoted themselves to their tea. This gave Sherlock Holmes an opportunity to clear his mind from the recent onslaught and speak.

"This is very serious, Mrs. Angel, and Mrs.Windibank," he said nodding to them respectively. Having done so he immediately looked up at Mrs. Hudson with a pleading look, seeking assurance that he had remembered which was which. She smiled and nodded. Holmes continued. "I will not keep you any longer here. You must be tired and the shock of what you have discovered has been very upsetting. I will assure you that I will do everything in my power to solve this mystery and find your children."

He again looked at Mrs. Hudson, and if begging for her intervention.

She responded perfectly on cue. "Let me see you ladies to the door and order you up a cab. Don't worry my dears, Mr. Holmes will look after the fare. Come please and let these two get to the task at hand of finding your children. Oh, and do leave me your address in London. Mr. Holmes will be getting back to you very soon and he will have to know where to find you."

With a talent I had not seen in her previously Mrs. Hudson kept chatting, not letting either Mrs. A or Mrs. W get a word in until they were up out of their chairs, out the door, down the stairs, and dispatched into a cab.

Holmes smiled as he gazed out of the window. "I do rather expect that there may be a surcharge on our rent next month. Do you agree, Watson?"

"If it is less than fifty pounds I would say you got off lightly."

Silence returned to the room as Mrs. Hudson cleared away the tea service.

"This is dreadful," said Holmes. "Those two who we re-united just days ago are now missing."

"Hmm, yes," I said. "Vanished."

"Indeed," added Mrs. Hudson, "without a trace."

Holmes looked up and glared at the two of us. I returned his look with the smile of a thousand year old Buddha. Mrs. Hudson assumed the face of the Sphinx. I could not wait for Holmes to leave and for the good lady and me to have a not-to-be-drinking-tea-at-the-same-time jolly laugh about it.

Sherlock Holmes was not amused. "If you two comedians will excuse me for an hour, I must send my Baker Street Irregulars to work. I may have to send Mycroft's as well. There is something very sinister going on here and I fear their children are not at all safe." With this he put on his ulster and hat and left.

I do not know at what hour Holmes returned to 221B Baker Street. I had retired for the night before he did so. My years, however, with the BEF in Afghanistan had forced me to be a light sleeper and I was awakened by the ringing of our bell at close to five o'clock on a Saturday morning. I jumped out of bed and pulled on my dressing gown and made my way to the stairs. Mrs. Hudson was already at the door and admitting Inspector Lestrade. He ascended the stairs and greeted me with a sullen nod. "Doctor Watson, would be so kind as to wake Mr. Holmes? I need both of you come with me at once."

Holmes appeared in the parlor, also in his gown. Both of us quickly dressed and returned to meet with the Inspector.

"Good morning, Inspector," said Holmes. "And what brings you to Baker Street at this early hour. I'm afraid I am already quite consumed with another case that may have significant implications to the nation." Sherlock Holmes usually took some subtle pleasure when Scotland Yard turned to him in desperation but there was no hint of *sangfroid* in his voice. The grim look on Lestrade's face made such a reaction unwelcome.

"We wouldn't be here if we didn't need you, Holmes," said Lestrade. "You bloody well know that. There's been a murder. Two of them in fact. A young man and woman. Over by Fenchurch Street. It's a ghastly site. Very nasty."

"All murder is nasty," came Holmes's rejoinder. "What is it about this one?"

"They were decapitated. He cut their heads off and just left the bodies. There's no blood around so it must have happened elsewhere and then the bodies were dumped in the lane."

"That's terrible," I blurted. "Another Jack the Ripper attack?"

"No. Impossible," said Lestrade.

"How can you say that?" I challenged. "That fellow has not hit for awhile. He may have wanted to do something a little different this time around."

The heads of both Lestrade and Holmes turned to me at the same time and their voices came in unison. "He's dead."

The tone of the voice and the look I was given told me to be silent and not ask any more questions.

"Oh," was all I said.

"Very well," said Holmes. "Tell me more. What else did you see? Have you kept your men away from the bodies?"

"Of course. We're not completely incompetent, as much as you would like to believe we are. I searched their bodies for any papers, any type of identification. I have their names, but nothing else yet."

"Very well," said Holmes. "Who are they?"

"They're a young married couple. Names are Mary and Hosmer Angel. They had travel tickets in their pockets. Here," Lestrade said to Holmes as he handed over a small set of papers. Holmes did not reach out his hand to take them. He did not reply. I looked at him and saw the blood drain from his face. I have observed Sherlock Holmes in many situations where his life was in danger but I had never seen him look as if he were about to faint. He put his hand to the back of a chair for support and then with some awkwardness sat down. He lowered his head into his hands and shook it slowly.

"Good heavens Holmes; what's the problem?" said Lestrade. "I've arrived here a score of times with stories of finding bodies. Never seen you react like this before."

Holmes looked up and stood up slowly. "They were my clients, Inspector. They had come to me and it was my duty to protect them."

"Well then, they won't be needing your protection any more Holmes," said Lestrade brusquely. "Ours neither. We're Scotland Yard, Holmes, and we're supposed to be protecting all of Great Britain. Every day one of our clients gets killed. It's called failure, Holmes. Welcome to the club."

Holmes looked at Lestrade and then reached for a card on the side table. In a voice just above a whisper, he said, "Their mothers are both staying at this address. They will be able to give firm identification. Please have one of your men go and bring them to the scene. And please send one who has at least a modicum of sensitivity and tack. It will be a very painful mission."

As we descended the stairs and entered on to Baker Street I saw something that again I had never seen in Sherlock Holmes. There was a tear, several tears in fact, trickling down his face.

"Lestrade," said Holmes, "please have your driver take a short detour via Westminster. There is someone else who must be told."

Lestrade looked at Holmes. "This is bigger than just a crazy serial killer, is what I believe you are telling me."

"Possibly much bigger," said Holmes.

The police carriage hurried through the deserted streets of London. In the late fall there was a bitter cold dampness to the air. I could imagine two mothers being told that their children were dead and being brought through the miserable chilly streets of London to identify their headless bodies. A part of my heart died that moment in sympathy with them.

At Westminster Holmes descended from the carriage and walked slowly towards the entry. After being cleared by the guard he entered. It was a full fifteen minutes before he returned.

"I am sorry to have delayed you, Inspector," he said humbly. "But that had to be done. Mycroft had to know."

Lestrade said nothing, and just gave a small nod.

Fenchurch is all the way across the City and past St. Paul's. With the streets empty we arrived in less than twenty minutes. Holmes and Lestrade and a couple of his men began walking towards a laneway. I followed. I looked into the lane and froze. The two mothers were coming out, holding on to each other for support.

Holmes stiffened and then walked towards them resolutely, knowing that he had failed to protect their children. "Mrs. Windibank, and Mrs. Angel, I cannot tell you how deeply sorry I am. . ." That was as far as he got in his words of condolence that I was sure he had been rehearsing all the way since Westminster.

"Mr. Holmes," interrupted Mrs. Angel, "may we have a word with you. And please you too, Doctor Watson."

"Yes, please," said Mrs. Windibank. "We must speak with you."

One of these country ladies grabbed Holmes by the sleeve of his coat, and the other grabbed me and led us back out onto the pavement by Fenwick Street.

Mrs. Angel looked directly into the face of Sherlock Holmes. "Mr. Holmes," she said, "what we saw back in the lane was terrible and horrible to look at and my heart goes out to whoever will be affected by it, but those are not our children."

For once Mrs. Windibank did not repeat what had just been said even though Holmes waited for her to do so. Hearing nothing from her he spoke in the low and gentle voice that he is capable of summoning when tragedy and necessity require it. "My dear ladies, what you saw was beyond doubt a devastating blow to both of you. I am deeply sorry, and I know that you must be in shock . . ." Again he was not allowed to finish his sentence.

"Mr. Holmes," said Mrs. Windibank. "Please listen to us. We are the mothers of our children. We know what their bodies look like head or not. Those are not our children. We are in deep shock at what we saw but we and not so far gone that we cannot tell that whoever those poor souls are, they are not related to us."

Holmes looked intently at both of him and they looked just as intently back at him. "Please permit me to ask," he said respectfully. "How it is that you are so sure of what you have just said?"

"Their hands," said Mrs. Angel.

"Yes, their hands," repeated Mrs. Windibank. "My daughter was fair-skinned. You have seen her. There is not a freckle on her body. That young woman, whoever she may be, and my heart goes out to her mother, is covered with them."

"My son," continued Mrs. Angel, "has long slender fingers. That young man has hands like bear paws and fingers like sausages. Bratwurst. And he is far heavier and larger than my son. The man, bless his soul, is not my son."

Holmes nodded at both of them. "If you will excuse me ladies, I must go and confirm what you have just told me. And you have my assurance that I will not rest until your children are safely restored to you." He turned and entered the laneway. I followed.

5 THE RUGBY HEAD COUPLE

Holmes approached the bodies and knelt beside them while a constable held a torch to provide light. The pieces of canvas covering the tops of the bodies were removed and the gory sight of their bloody necks was revealed. The heads had been severed quite cleanly, indicating either a sword or an ax and a powerful single blow. As Lestrade had told us, there was little blood on the ground around them. There was also little blood on their clothes. They were both dressed in evening wear, not of the most expensive kind but acceptably fashionable. Holmes gently prodded at various parts of the body, managing as he always did to show complete respect to the corpse yet at the same time working to discern any possible clues that might be gleaned.

"Please," he said. "You may take them to the morgue. There is nothing more that can be learned here. Thank you Inspector. I expect that by noon hour we should be able to identify those two poor unfortunate souls."

"You are quite certain Holmes," said Lestrade," that they are not the Angels. They were most certainly carrying the identification papers of Mary and Hosmer Angel."

"There are many things I do not yet know about this case," Holmes answered. "But of that I am very sure. These poor souls, whoever they were, have been gruesomely murdered by some fiend who clearly intends to deceive and to lead us to believe that Mr. and Mrs. Angel are dead. The ghastly decapitation is intended to make it appear as if it is the work of Jack the Ripper, which we know it cannot possibly be. Why these events have taken place I do not yet know but am determined to discover. I met both Mr. and Mrs. Angel howbeit briefly but I am positive that these two are not they. So are the mothers of Mr. and Mrs. Angel. That should be sufficient evidence for you Inspector."

"If you say so, Mr. Holmes," returned Lestrade. "At the moment, however, the names on their documents are all we have and that is what I must release. If you could let us know as soon as you deduce who they really are we will give the rightful ones. Of course if you could find the real Mr. and Mrs. Angel that would help us as well. Good-day Mr. Holmes; Doctor Watson." Lestrade turned and left Holmes and me on the pavement of Fenchurch Street.

"Bodies usually require heads in order to be positively identified, Holmes. How are you going to go about discerning who these two are?"

"Elementary, my dear Watson. They were both wearing matching wedding rings so it is almost certain that they were married to each other. The male is an enormous, athletic young man. Sixteen or maybe even seventeen stone and not a bit of fat on his body. The hair on the sides of his head is shaved unfashionably short. His lower legs show recent signs of small cuts, abrasions, and bruising. His hands are heavily calloused. A gentleman who plays sports may have large powerful hands but the palms remain soft. A workingman's become hardened. There is only one place, or should I say one position, that a man that athletic and large could have acquired those physical attributes. And with your knowledge of the sporting world I am quite sure that even you could come to a logical conclusion once you had observed those facts."

I thought for a moment. "He is too large to be a footballer, and much too that way for cricket. I would guess he is a rugby player. Most likely a forward, one who plays prop in the scrum. That reduces our possible candidates to a few thousand; maybe a few hundred if we think he is a member of a Rugby Union team."

"Excellent, my good doctor," said Holmes. "Now, we add to that that his skin, those parts that might have been exposed to the sun, was still bearing a tan. Players in England never get a tan in our miserable wet climate so he has been somewhere recently where it was warm and the sun was shining."

"One of the team who just came back from Australia and New Zealand? That would make sense."

"Ah, yes it would. And the only one who will not be showing up for practice today. Now then, how difficult will it be to establish his identify?"

"We should have his identity by supper time," said I.

"I was rather hoping to have it before finishing lunch," replied Holmes. "I suggest that we just locate the team captain and ask him about his players."

"Very sorry, Holmes, but that cannot be done," I answered.

"And why not?" he queried me, a touch imperiously.

"He's dead. Robert Seddon was the chap's name. Drowned whilst on the tour. Fell out of a boat and couldn't swim."

"Very well then, can we locate the manager? Please do not tell me that he also drowned."

"No. He's fine. His name is Alfred Shaw. In fact he spends most of his time playing cricket, and took on the Rugby team tour as a special venture. But I have a hunch were we might be able to find him."

"Very good, Watson. And just where, pray tell would we find an enthusiastic cricket player who has just returned from the Antipodes with a Rugby Union team?"

"Lord's Cricket Ground would be a good place to start," I replied. I had been to the place many times as it was only a few minute's walk from Baker Street. Holmes had never been there but with his encyclopedic knowledge of London he certainly knew where it was.

Alfred Shaw had often been described by the sporting press as "larger than life." Whether this was true or not it was undeniable that he was louder than life. By mid-morning we had found him in the club house at Lord's. Like many sporting men he was also an avid reader of my stories in *The Strand* and quite pleased to meet Sherlock Holmes in person and to know that he might have a part to play in solving a mystery.

Our conversation began with some idle chat about the recent tour of the team. I had to carry this part of our meeting since other than knowing that there had been a tour, Sherlock Holmes had not bothered to read anything at all about it as he considered all sporting past-times to have little relevance to intriguing and diabolical crime. On all other occasions in the past he had been right. Today, however, was different and I was pleased – very well, I will admit that I might have felt a little bit smug – that he had to depend on me. Holmes sat in silence for the first short while and tried to look interested as Mr. Shaw and I chatted about the highlights of the tour.

To my relief Shaw turned to Sherlock Holmes after a mercifully short few minutes and said, "Right. Now I could sit here and talk rugby, or cricket, or football all day long, gentlemen, but I rather suspect that Mr. Sherlock Holmes did not come here for that reason. I would suspect that you, Mr. Holmes sir, must be investigating something untoward about our tour. Were some of the lads taking money under the table? We were very strict about all members being amateurs, and not a one could take a farthing. No? Well then I will wager it was the wagering. Thousands of pounds were wagered on the games and it would not be the first time that a player or two took a bit on the side and deliberately let the other side win so as to please the gamblers. Mind you, that would be much more likely to have been some of the New Zealand lads, since our boys beat them every time, except for the Auckland squad. Or do you believe that one of my lads threw that game? Can't say as I saw anything that would have led me to think that. Far as I could see those sheep herders were just lucky, that's all. Right from the start . . ." I am quite sure that Mr. Shaw would have recounted in detail every play of the game had we permitted him to carry on down that track. Holmes, respectfully but effectively cut him off.

"Not at all sir. Not at all. We are here for a much more serious reason than the fixing of a Rugby match."

"Really, Mr. Holmes. For the life of me I cannot think of much that could be more serious than fixing an honest sporting match. I remember in 1847 we had three rascals . . ."

"Murder," interrupted Holmes. "There has been a murder. That is why we are here."

Alfred Shaw stopped speaking. The voluble gentleman stared at Holmes in open-mouthed shock.

"Not one of my boys, sir? Please do not say that one of my fellows has been killed. Please sir."

"Was there," queried Holmes, "a member of your squad who played, ah, what was it Watson?"

"A prop. Big fellow."

"Yes, a prop," continued Holmes. "A working man, with dark hair, and he was married to a red-haired woman who accompanied him on the tour."

"Why that would be Oswald and Roberta Whineray. Wonderful chap. His wife too. Couldn't find a nicer couple. And no, he was not from the gentlemen class, sir. He was a working class bloke that had a position down on the docks. Spent all day there when he wasn't on the field, lifting sacks and pallets. Strong as an ox it made him. Just a bull in a scrum. You're not saying that something has happened to him, has it? That would be terrible. He and Roberta were not married all that long and talking about starting a family and all. Is she alright? Does Roberta know that something might have happened to Ozzie?"

"The situation is very serious," said Holmes. "I am terribly sorry to be the bearer of tragic news, but it appears that they may both have been the victims of foul play. I know that such news will be very disturbing to you, sir, but I beg you, please compose yourself and tell me everything you possibly can about what may have taken place in the lives of this unfortunate young couple in the past few weeks. If you could manage to do that sir it will be a great help to me, and to Scotland Yard, and to their families."

The sportsman said nothing and I could see that the color had gone out of his face. Twice he tried to speak and could not get the words out. He stood and in a whisper excused himself, saying that he would come back to us in a few minutes. I watched as he walked towards the door of the clubhouse and stood by looking out on to the cricket pitch, alone.

Mr. Shaw remained alone on the edge of the field for a full ten minutes. I knew that Sherlock Holmes was impatient to extract every possible bit of data from him as quickly as possible. Yet I had also observed in Sherlock Holmes a rigid discipline in dealing with people. Friendliness and compassion, he had often said, along with generosity loosed more tongues than demands and orders ever did. Holmes waited and said nothing until Mr. Shaw returned.

He sat down across from Holmes and spoke quietly. "Ozzie Whineray was a lad from the east end of London. Just a big, happy boy. Not the sharpest knife in the drawer but a large convivial boy who was always ready to laugh and sing over a pint at the pub. He met Roberta – as far as I know she was a barmaid in Whitechapel – and they were married two years ago. The majority of our team were young gentlemen who came from wealthy families and could easily afford to come on a tour for five months.

"Ozzie and Roberta had no money at all but they decided to come anyway for the love of the game and knowing that they would most likely never again have such an opportunity. I tried to arrange to give them what we call broken-time payment to replace the wages he would lose from being on the team, but the Directors of the Union are very strict. No payment whatsoever is allowed. Everyone must remain strictly amateur. That wasn't a problem on the tour. Some of the wealthier lads were true gentlemen and they made sure that any bills at the pub or in the restaurants were discreetly looked after. No one talked about it; it was just what was done. The captain, Bob Seddon, he was as fine a young gentleman as I have ever met. God bless him. He quietly put the arm on some of the other young gents who had ample funds and they made sure that the working lads were looked after.

"Of course when we all got back to London a few weeks ago the boys from working class homes were in a very tight spot as they had not been able to earn their wages for months on end, so they were all scrambling to find something to do to earn a quick quid or two. I had thought that Ozzie would just ask for more hours on the docks – he was not opposed to doing a double shift for a week or two – and get themselves back on their feet that way but Ozzie had a different opportunity.

"He came to me soon a few days back and told me about a strange meeting he had with some chap who had offered him a hundred quid. Said this fellow came and told him he was acting on behalf of the family of Mrs. Hosmer Angel. She and her husband were on the tour as well. Not as part of the team but she was the writer for the *Rugby Union News* and Hosmer worked for Thomas Cook's and did all the travel arrangements. The two couples had become somewhat friendly with each other on the tour."

"That is quite understandable," said Holmes. "What was this offer? Please tell me as much about it as you can remember."

"Well sir, I thought it a bit odd but there was good money in it and goodness knows Ozzie and Bobbie needed it. Ozzie told me that this chap told him that some aged great uncle of Mary's, Mrs. Angel that is, had just arrived in London from New Zealand and wanted to see his grand niece before he passed on. He was over eighty years old and had no other family. Not in good health and pretty much blind. But then Hosmer and Mary had just missed him because both of them had just taken assignments to return to New Zealand and were already on their way. The chap tells Ozzie that it would break the old man's heart if he couldn't see his niece before he died seeing as he had come this way and it would be terrible if he had come to England from Auckland to see her only to have her be on a boat headed out the day before he arrives.

"So he said that as a friend of the family he thought it would be a fine thing to do to have someone, another couple that is, pretend that they were Hosmer and Mary and spend some time with the old fellow and that it would bring just a lot of joy into his life before he passed on to the other side, as they say.

"Well now Ozzie was a bit of a humble fellow and he didn't know if he could pull that off but the chap says he wants him and Bobbie to do it because they were just on the tour with Hosmer and Mary and would be able to talk about it realistically. And besides, the old fellow's real interest was in his niece and Bobbie having been a barmaid had lots of practice pretending as barmaids have to do with all sorts of blokes they would prefer to throw their ale at and kick them out the door.

"So Ozzie and Bobbie pretended they were Hosmer and Mary and went and visited this old man, and they had a nice little meeting and the old boy was happy and Ozzie had a hundred quid and could pay their back rent and everything is just fine. At least for awhile."

"Ah, and then something happened?" queried Holmes.

"Well now, Ozzie is such a friendly lad that he would never suspect anyone of not being on the up and up with him But Bobbie, she's been working in the pub serving men since she was sixteen years old and, well, as they say, she's been around. She's a fun lass and friendly but you wouldn't be able to pull the wool over her eyes, as they say. She gets it in her head that something is not right about this whole arrangement and she doesn't quite trust this chap who says he's a friend of Mary's family. She and Mary, they got pretty close as two young married women will do when they're traveling on tour with their husbands, and something about the whole thing didn't sit right with her.

"So Ozzie came to me – I gather he sort of thought of me as a father type advisor as I am quite a few years older and managed the tour and all – and he asks me what he should do. And I ask him what is it that was upsetting Bobbie. He says that during this meeting they had together with the old man, Mary's great Uncle Peter, Peter Sutherland his name was, that the old fellow puts a stack of papers on the table and says that these are for Mary. He has no other family and so he is handling over his wealth to her. And then he has a document in his pocket and he gives it to her to sign saying as she has received them. Well now, Bobbie wasn't expecting anything like that and was caught off guard and so she signs it, writing Mary's name. And then the old boy puts the document back in his pocket without bothering to look at it seeing as he is nearly blind, and smiles and says that he had a great load off his mind and that all of his affairs are now in order. And he can go to his eternal reward in peace.

"When they get out of the meeting, the chap who hired them to pretend they were Hosmer and Mary is waiting for them and he takes the papers they were given saying that he will look after them for the family and he pays them their hundred quid and throws in another twenty for good measure and assures them that Hosmer and Mary will be so grateful to them for standing in for them and would have been so very disappointed when they learned that Uncle Peter had come to London to see them and they missed him. And everything seems just fine.

"Well now, Bobbie, she doesn't mind acting and pretending but she knows that it is against the law to sign another person's name. She knows that it's forgery, and she gets more and more uncomfortable about it as the day goes by. She also had a bit of a look at the papers they were given and she knows that they are certificates for stocks and bonds and bank deposits and such. Now Ozzie, he wouldn't know a stock certificate from a score card but Bobbie has seen a lot of them passed back and forth between gentlemen who do their business in the pub as many do. So she thinks that there may be something a bit on the sketchy side going on here. She tells Ozzie that she is ready to go and talk to someone at Scotland Yard about it because she's an honest lass and doesn't want anyone to think she was a forger and such.

"Ozzie, he tells her not to do anything yet. He doesn't want to risk the hundred and twenty pounds he's just been paid for an hour's work. So he says he'll go and find the chap that hired them and ask about it and get it all sorted out. That's what he told me he had decided when we talked just a couple of days back. So I have to suppose that's what he did and that was the last I saw of him, Mr. Holmes."

"That has been very helpful. Thank you Mr. Shaw," said Holmes in return. "May I ask about this chap who said he was a friend of the family? What else might young Mr. Oswald have said concerning him? Please try to remember and tell me exactly as you can, sir."

Mr. Shaw looked thoughtful for a minute. "I cannot say much as I never met or saw the man. Ozzie said he was older than I am, so I would think maybe in his fifties. Tall. Came across as very intelligent, very knowledgeable, and very polished. Perfectly dressed with a very expensive coat, suit and hat and all. Very charming. But there was one incident that Ozzie thought rather odd."

"And what, pray tell was that?" said Holmes.

"Well now, at the entrance to the rugby field where we practice; that was where the chap meet with Ozzie the first time; there's a big old friendly mongrel dog, Punch we call him, that has staked out his territory near to the gate. He's been there for several years. Just a big old friendly cur that comes up to you and nuzzles you as dogs do. And we all give the old fellow a friendly pat and rub his head as we go by and if we have a treat, a bit of lunch leftover and such, we give it to him.

"Ozzie said he watched as this chap walked out of the gate. Punch comes up and nuzzles him and doesn't the man raise his stick and brings it down terrible hard on the old dog's front leg and breaks it. The poor old mongrel is in pain and whining and the man just walks on. We learn later that the leg is shattered and that the old thing has to be put down. It was very sad. The rest of us didn't know what had happened but Ozzie saw it and it troubled him. Said he couldn't imagine anyone connected to Mary's family being so cruel and heartless in that way."

"Yes, that was a surprisingly cruel thing to do," said Holmes. "Did this man have a name that he gave to Ozzie?"

"Oh I am sure he did, but not one that Ozzie told me. Said he was some sort of professor at Cambridge or something like that. But that's all he said, to me at least."

"Is there anything else, anything else at all you can remember, Mr. Shaw? Please, it is frightfully important," asked Holmes.

"No. If I do I will send a note back to you straightaway," said Shaw. "It is very sad you know. Such a triumphal tour it was and we should all be celebrating. What with Bob Seddon drowning and now this, it's become something tragic. The rest of the boys will be very upset when they hear about this."

"It is only to be expected that they will," said Holmes. "They have lost a friend. Please tell them not to believe anything they read about it in the press."

Alfred Shaw gave a questioning look to Sherlock Holmes. "I will tell them that sir. By your words I suspect that there is a deeper story to all this than you have told me."

"Indeed there is," said Holmes. "In due time it will be revealed and, if it at all within my power, justice will be done."

We thanked the affable sportsman and, as Baker Street was close by, we started our return there on foot.

"Alright, Holmes," I said. "Out with it. Who is this mysterious professor that appears to be behind all this?"

"At the moment," he replied. "I am not at all certain. I have heard through my contacts that a man fitting the description has emerged as a very powerful figure in the network of crime that has crept over the Continent and all of England. Very little is known about him and he has never been so much as brought in for questioning by Scotland Yard. However, I will contact all of my agents, and set my Irregulars to work to find out whatever can be known. I may even have to ask Mycroft to help by using his spies. However, there is nothing else I can do concerning him presently, so we will follow the path that is open to us and try to find this old Uncle Peter."

"And just how do you plan to do that," I asked.

Holmes stopped walking and gave his head a bit of a sideways nod. "If I can tolerate it, we shall have to meet with the mothers again. They very likely could tell us immediately."

6 UNCLE PETER

We did not return to Baker Street but hailed a cab and made our way to Number 31 Lyon Place in Camberwell where the mothers had taken over the rooms of their missing children. We had had a very early start on the morning and it had just gone half-past ten when we arrived there. It was a modest rooming house and the landlady ushered us into the sitting room while she went to fetch the mothers.

When they appeared I immediately offered our apologies as it was evident that they had gone back to their beds after such an early and shocking start to their morning.

"It is not a problem at all, Dr. Watson. We are eager to hear if you have any news of our children."

"Yes. Have you found out anything this morning, Mr. Holmes?"

"We have made just a little progress," said Holmes. "I will not give you false comfort. I am deeply concerned that your children may be in peril. However we will not cease to search for them until they are found. We have again disturbed you this morning as I believe you may have some additional information that will be useful to us in our quest."

"What is it you wish to know, Mr. Holmes?"

"If there is any way at all that we can help, Mr. Holmes, just ask us."

"They are, after all, our children."

"We are their mothers."

"Ah yes, you are indeed," said Holmes. "I need to know about this man, Uncle Peter. Who is he and what brought him to London? It would be perhaps a bit more efficient if just one of you were to tell me the whole story. Please."

"Oh yes, well then Mrs. Angel should tell you. She has more schooling than I do and is quite the gifted story-teller."

"Goodness gracious, Mrs. Windibank, you are the one who is the relative of Uncle Peter, not I. It is incumbent on you to tell Mr. Holmes what you know, not me."

"Oh, well thank you my dear, but you really are far better suited . . ."

"Ladies," interrupted Holmes. "Mrs. Windibank, Mrs. Angel is quite correct. As you are the relative to Uncle Peter I would ask you to pass on the information."

"Oh very well. But I am not a blood relative, you know, only by marriage and twice removed."

"That, I assure you," countered Holmes, "still makes you a relative. Please. Proceed."

"Uncle Peter as we call him is Mr. Peter Sutherland. He is the uncle of my first husband, Russell Sutherland, who, bless his soul, was a wonderful husband and father to my daughter Mary but he has been dead these past five years and I have remarried, to Mr. Windibank, which is why my name is now Mrs. Windibank. He is somewhat younger than me, but that is another story. Younger husbands can be useful from time to time. But that is most likely not the information you are interested in is it, Mr. Holmes? Very well. Peter Sutherland left England as a young man nearly sixty years ago and immigrated to Australia. He resided I am told in Botany Bay for his first few years and then, as they say down there, he crossed the ditch and took up residence in New Zealand. Now there are no more than half a million people living in New Zealand, all good British stock mind you, but they do have well over twenty million sheep.

"Now Peter Sutherland, at least as far as I have been told, had no interest in being a sheep herder, so he set up a business managing the importing and exporting of wool. He was quite good and worked hard and, so I am told, had the entire trade. Then just a few years ago, when he was over seventy years old, he was the first to invest in shipping frozen beef and lamb from New Zealand. As you know that business is growing by leaps and bounds every day. Last year he turned eighty years old and he sold most of his interests, except, of course, so I am told, the reefer boats – that is what they call those ships –and he came back to London to put his final affairs in order."

I interrupted her involuntarily at this point. "He must be an enormously wealthy man. Over fifty years of managing the wools shipments and a decade of reefers!"

"Oh yes, doctor. Peter Sutherland is one of the richest men in the Antipodes. His estate, what with the reefer business mind you, will be worth at least half a million pounds. He is very wealthy indeed."

"You said that he put his affairs in order," said Holmes. "Why was it necessary to come to London to do that?"

"Oh, because my daughter, Mary, is his only living relative. He was a bachelor all his life. I gather that is why he ended up so wealthy. Married to his business, he was. I had corresponded with him quite faithfully and had told him that Mary had grown up to be a responsible young woman and was now married and, along with her husband, Hosmer, was doing quite well for herself. He was pleased to hear that and wrote that he felt quite at peace in leaving his estate and his shipping business to the two of them. It was always in his will to leave his estate to Mary but now he declared he was at peace about it, yes. He was at peace.'""

"They will be one of the richest young couples in England," I exclaimed. "I am amazed that they were just living as they were and seeking to establish careers. They have a life of leisure ahead of them."

"Doctor Watson," Mrs. Windibank said a bit sharply. "My dear friend Mrs. Angel and I are sensible, God-fearing women and we were not about to let our children become spoiled lazy toffs like all those sons and daughters of the dukes and earls. We expected them to earn their own living and do a decent days work for a fair wage. Did we not, Mrs. Angel?"

"Indeed we did. No children of ours were going to be parasites, living off the backs of the working people. The two of them will come into money soon enough. We wanted to be certain, before God we did, that our children were not raised to be idle layabouts."

"Are you telling me then that Mrs. and Mrs. Angel had no idea that they were the sole recipients of Mr. Sutherland's fortune?" asked Holmes.

"That is quite correct sir. Mary, my daughter that is, had been led to believe that he had left his estate to the New Zealand Society for the Protection of the Kiwi Bird and other such charities and that he had become highly patriotic towards New Zealand and so all his money would remain there. She expected nothing and yet had warm feeling towards him as he was her father's uncle and part of her family."

"Yet she was in New Zealand earlier this year. Did she not see him at that time?" asked Holmes.

"It was unusual, but no, she did not," replied the girl's mother. "It had been planned and hoped for but Uncle Peter had taken ill and had been sent over to Melbourne to convalesce. She tried to take time off while the team was in Sydney but he had to undergo some minor surgery and her visit had to be cancelled. It was just one disappointment after another and so they never met. That was also part of the reason he came to London. But then she and Hosmer took off on their strange journeys back to New Zealand just before he arrived. Fortunately, with your help Mr. Holmes, they found each other and we reached them by post and told them about Uncle Peter's arrival, and they arranged to go and see him. I assume that the meeting took place but as we have not heard from them I do not know for sure."

Sherlock Holmes stood up and abruptly ended the conversation.

"Excuse me, ladies," he said. "I am sure that there is much more I could learn but time has become very pressing. It is of vital importance that we locate and speak to this Uncle Peter immediately. Could you please tell me where he can be found?"

"Oh, he spends much of his day at the Reform Club. It's on Pall Mall I believe."

"Do you know the Reform Club, Mr. Holmes? It's the place that Mr. Phineas Fogg began his wonderful journey from. The one Mr. Dickens told us all about."

"No my dear. That was not Mr. Dickens. It was that Frenchie fellow, Mr. Jules Verne."

"Oh yes. The Frenchie. But it was the Reform Club all the same."

"Yes. The Reform Club on Pall Mall. I believe it is near Buckingham Palace."

"Ah, yes," said Holmes. "Pall Mall is near the Palace. Thank you for helping us with that." He then turned to me and said, "Come Watson. There is no time to waste."

We hailed a cab in Camberwell and Holmes offered the driver a generous enhancement to the fare if he would break every regulation of the streets of London. He obliged and did so.

"We certainly now have a motive for murder," said Holmes and we bounced along over Vauxhall Bridge. "Half a million pounds has been the cause of minor wars between nations. Some very patient criminal or a syndicate of criminals has been plotting this enormous theft for some time. Watson, you and I must now divide and conquer. May I impose upon you my good doctor to carry on to the Reform Club and see if you can locate this Uncle Peter chap? I will be dropped off at Westminster and pay a visit to Mycroft. When half a million pounds worth of negotiable securities are about to be circulating through London I must, even if not altogether willingly, call in reinforcements."

The driver stopped on Abingdon and Sherlock Holmes alighted and crossed over into Westminster. I continued on to Pall Mall. The porter at the door of the Reform Club greeted me and on learning that I was Dr. John Watson, the author of all those wonderful detective stories about Sherlock Holmes, and that I was making a visit on a Saturday morning, was quite pleased to show me in. The General Secretary of the Club was called and he led me into one of the sitting rooms. "It is a delight to have such an interesting visitor, Dr. Watson. We subscribe to *The Strand* and the men enjoy reading all your splendid stories. In fact we have ten subscriptions to *The Strand* and we can never keep the copies on hand. Our members keep pinching them. And you, my good man, are entirely to blame. Our staff are about to serve a lovely luncheon. It is quite a popular event on a Saturday you know. The wives are only too eager to shoo the husbands out of the house and the men are only too happy to oblige. It would be most interesting if you could join us. It would just the type of event that the chaps would thoroughly enjoy. It would make their day, I dare say."

"Ah, you are very kind to offer," I said graciously. "However I must decline. I am in the midst of helping Mr. Holmes with some research on the criminal temperament and there is a visiting guest at the Club who he has asked me to interview. It is a rather confidential matter. The dear old fellow was once a guest of Her Majesty in Botany Bay but seems to have had an upright and prosperous life ever since he paid his debt to society. I'm sure that it would not do to alert your regular members to that. Would you not agree?"

"Most understandable," said the Secretary. "No doubt you are referring to old Mr. Peter Sutherland. He arrived in London just a few weeks ago and has been quite the entertaining story teller since then. Not at all ashamed of his time in Botany Bay all those years ago. Been regaling the chaps here with all sorts of fabulous tales. Although I must confess to you sir," he said lowering his voice to *sotto voce,* 'that there are quite of few of our chaps who have seen the inside of one of Her Majesty's special residences and have gone on to earn their fortune. The other clubs up and down Pall Mall are far too snobbish to allow them in, but we at the Reform Club rather enjoy the spirit of the adventure that they bring. A bit on the non-conformist side we are. Quite the lot of lovable old rascals we have here, if you know what I mean."

"And for that reason," I replied, "among many others, you have the reputation as the liveliest Club on the Mall. So would it be possible for you to arrange a place for Mr. Sutherland and me to have a private chat? And perhaps your staff could bring a little refreshment?"

"Of course sir," he replied. "Please come this way."

He led me to a comfortable but small sitting room. A few minutes later he re-appeared followed by an elderly gentleman who was supported by a cane in one hand and the arm of one of the young stewards on the other. He was stooped over, thin and gaunt. His face looked a bit on the pasty side and his eyes somewhat clouded, but and he beamed a smile at me, friendly even if his teeth had long since ceased to gleam or even be entirely present.

After being introduced by the porter the old chap sat down and in a voice still quite loud, as is common among those whose hearing is failing, said, "So you're the one who has been writing all those stories about that Sherlock Holmes fellow. Can't read them anymore. Can't see well enough. But there's always some young lad around who will read them to me. For a shilling or two mind you. But they're a welcome change from having to listen to some poor lad read lawyers letters and yet another miserable bond perspective. Wonderful stories, sir. Right glad to meet you doctor."

"Well thank you, Mr. Sutherland. Sherlock Holmes had heard of you and that you were in London and he is most interested to learn about you, sir. You had a bit of a rough start to your life but you have done wonderfully well ever since. Mr. Holmes, as you may know sir, is quite the expert on criminal justice as well as being England's finest consulting detective. He's writing a bit of a monograph on the effectiveness of our prison systems. Not much good coming out of them these days but everyone has an opinion on how to better the system. But as he is of a scientific bent, sir, he wants evidence of what has and has not worked. Your life is a wonderful example of what did work. So he is most anxious that he learn about Mr. Peter Sutherland."

"Ha. Indeed. Right, now I am flattered indeed doctor. So you ask away. At this point in my life I have nothing more to gain nor lose. We Kiwis don't put much store in past reputations, as many of us have some skeletons in the closet. Not as bad as the Aussies of course. They have more than skeletons in their closets and those that don't well they just don't bother with the closets. Right there out in the open those blokes are. So you just go ask away and if I live long enough to make it into one of your stories I would be right proud. Trying to put my affairs in order I am now and knowing that I might end up in a story about Sherlock Holmes would give me just a little something more to present to St. Peter when I arrive at the pearly gates."

"Oh good heavens, sir," I replied with a chuckle. "I don't believe that being connected to Sherlock Holmes is going to do any of us any good in the great beyond. But do tell me your story all the same. I don't think it will do you any harm at least. I have my pencil and notepad at the ready"

The old fellow smiled. "Shall I 'Begin at the beginning and go on till you come to the end: then stop?' That's what the King demanded. Would that do for Sherlock Holmes?"

"Most assuredly, sir."

"Right then. All the chaps here already know that I was once a guest of Her Gracious Majesty in Botany Bay. They know because I now wear that as a badge of honor. Didn't feel that way about it sixty years ago, mind you. It was a right bad thing back then. But when I was just nineteen years old I relieved a gentleman's house of some of his silverware. He had more than he needed and I was on the hungry side. Course I didn't know what to do with it after I'd taken it so I tried to sell it to a pawn shop and the pawnbroker tells me to come back the next day and he'll have the money for me. So I go back the next day and takes the money and two constables are waiting there and next thing I know I'm in the jail, and then in front of the judge, and then on a ship to Botany Bay where I have to spend the next seven years wondering how I could have been so stupid. Are you with me so far, doctor?"

I was scribbling furiously. "Yes. Yes. Off to Australia to join the convicts you were. Pray, go on."

"Right. Well now first thing I learned is that if you're going to survive in that miserable place you can't do it all by yourself. A man has to have a mate and you have to look out for each other. So I found another young lad who had done something as stupid as I had, George Windibank was his name, and he and I became great mates. Together we put our backs together and fought off any blighters who crossed us and after seven years we were out of the convict zone and free.

"Now the second thing I learned was that you can live a life of crime and make a fair pile of quid without working and without paying taxes, or you can sleep in your own bed at night and be at peace. But you can't do both. So Georgie and I we decided that we would make our fortune all honest like and so we tried every opportunity that the Aussies offered us. We joined a whaling ship and damned if it did not nearly kill us both several times over. If it wasn't by drowning it was by freezing, and if it wasn't that then it was by getting crushed between a whale and a dinghy, or a dinghy and the ship. Right terrible work it was sir. Compared to it, the convict zone was Piccadilly. We worked in fear of our lives everyday thinking that we were going to get a handsome payment at the end but because we were the lowest fellows on the ladder our share was a miserable one sixty-forth of the profits and we had no more than would be gone in a month even if we near-starved ourselves. So we had had enough of that.

"We heard that there was good work in New Zealand. They were still fighting the natives over there and a couple of blokes who were willing to work hard could make a fortune or so we were told. So over we went and found work right away helping to herd sheep we did. Now I suppose you've heard that story from the Holy Writ about there being ninety-nine sheep what came safely home to the fold and one was lost. Well now sir, that story's a lie. Sheep are the stupidest animals on God's green earth. The true story is that ninety-nine got lost and only one was smart enough to find its way home. Georgie and I, we chased those stupid things from the north of Hawk's Bay to the south. We set aside a little money though and bought our own land and stock but after a few years of that we looked at each other and we said 'Chasing these stupid things may be alright if you're a Scot or an Irish man, but we're Englishmen, and there is no way under Providence that we're going to spend our lives with this nonsense.' So we sold out, at a tidy profit mind you. And then we went looking for gold for we heard that some bloke had found it near Westport in the Buller River. So off we went and blimey if we didn't find some and made a few quid, or I suppose I should say a few hundred quid, enough to walk back into Auckland and pretend we were gentlemen. In the colonies you know of course no one cares who your great-grandsire was, if you have money then you're a gentleman.

"Then Georgie he wants to start being friendly with the city toffs who do nothing but sit in clubs all day, like you see all up and down Pall Mall here. And the next thing he's been collared by some comely young lass who sees his money. So he gets married and heads back to England. And I lost my mate. Right sad I was about that, but no use crying over split milk, so on I go. As for me, never had a wife and never wanted one. Always said that those who love children should have them, and us who have no use for the little blighters should never get married.

"I looked all up and down the islands. The Scots had established themselves in Dunedin and were raising sheep. I thought they were much too dour for me in those days. But did you hear that just this year past they built themselves a statue to Robbie Burns, that miserable drunken philandering poet of theirs. And did you hear that no sooner had they unveiled the blessed thing that some bloke all full of his Scotch looks and says, "Ooo, look will ye. Hasn't our Robbie goot hees back to tha kirk an hees face to tha poob?' Did you hear about that Doctor Watson?" He was laughing as he told me this.

I had heard about it. It was just the type of story that the English loved to tell about the Scots, that is when they were not quoting Samuel Johnson's dictionary entry about 'oats.' But I laughed along with him.

"Right, now I could see that from the harbor in Dunedin, and from Wellington, and from Christchurch, and from Auckland there were ships coming and going and they were sending out wool and bringing in all the refined clothes and goods from England. And I knew from being a sheep rancher that I got a pittance selling my wool compared to what I paid for my suitings. I could see that somebody was making money and I learned that it was the fellow they called the middle man, the chap that controlled all the coming and going.

"He didn't do any of the real work; he just passed things from one poor bloke who was working all day making things or growing things, to another poor bloke who was working all day selling things. So I decided to be a middle man. I used my savings from the gold fields and bought the licenses to control all the wool leaving the port of Auckland, and then every other harbor. And then I added to that all the lumber. And then all the freight coming in. And then I bought some interests in the gold fields, and in the new foundries and machine works. And then I expanded across the ditch and added all sorts of things coming and going from Australia.

"Ten years ago now we sent the first refrigerated ships bearing beef and lamb from Sydney and Auckland all the way to London. Those shipments have expanded fifty-fold since that time and are continuing to grow. My only regret is that I am now over eighty years of age and I will not be around long enough to see the transport of frozen beef and lamb and fish help move good food all over the globe, from those places that have it abundance to those who need it. There is more than enough food in to world to feed the world's people several times over. However, the food and the people who need it are not in the same place, but we are on our way Dr. Watson to ending the hunger of every soul on earth."

With this the old man sighed and paused. "I have to be content that I have done my part. Others who are younger and healthier than me will have to pick up the torch. My run has been a good one, but it has come to an end. I was very ill earlier this year and speaking frankly doctor, I do not expect to be around this time next year. So starting a few months back I liquidated almost all my properties, my contracts, my licenses, my patents and turned them into cash and negotiable shares.

"Right. I was so grateful that I could do that before I died. Had I not, my estate would have been tied up in the courts and those barracudas, those sharks, those greedy lawyers and judges would have eaten everything they could and held matters up for years. Did you ever read Dickens's *Bleak House,* doctor? He didn't exaggerate. No sir, he did not.

"Well now doctor," he said and then paused. "That's my story, short and simple. I've come to England to meet my only remaining blood relative, my great niece, Mrs. Mary Angel. She and her husband were in New Zealand and Australia from May until September and try as we might we could not arrange for our paths to cross. So I have come back home to England for the first time since I was removed from its shores sixty years ago so that I could meet her and pass on my assets for her to look after. Blood, they say, is thicker than water and my brother always stood by me when I was in trouble, so it's only fair that I should do the same for his grandchildren now that I'm in a position to do so.

"I met the young lady and her husband here a couple of weeks back. Had a nice chat about rugby and their visit to New Zealand. They were a little coarser than I imagined they might have been, bit then so was I and more so when I was their age. The young fellow is supposed to come by again later this afternoon."

"You say," I asked, "that you met your niece and her husband recently?" Holmes had told me not to reveal anything to the old man that would upset him, so I said nothing about his visitors' being imposters. I could only hope that this bizarre case would be solved and that the dear old chap could end his days in the peace he sought. "And how did they look upon your not so illustrious early life and consequent success."

"Oh, they were right proud of me. Shipping young convicts off to Australia isn't done any more. Hasn't been for a long time. Many of the early blokes died. But there were some of us who stayed on and prospered. Some began schools, another chap wrote novels, and one fellow started a theater. So for some of us the punishment worked. But then who is to say if we might not have done far better in a prison in England. No one really knows nor can they, doctor. Although that does not help your research or Mr. Holmes's monograph if I say that no one really knows what works and doesn't when it comes to criminal justice."

"Even knowing that much is important," I assured him. "And on behalf of Sherlock Holmes I cannot thank you enough for imparting your story and your insights. I have no doubt it will appear, at least in summary form, in his monograph."

There was one very queer item that he mentioned in passing that I had to find some way to uncover further. "Your mate, George Windibank, how did he make out once he returned t England? Did he prosper in the same way you did?"

"Georgie? No not at all. His wife spent all his money and in their later years they lived very modestly. He had a son quite late on. Called him George after his father. But by the time Georgie died about ten years back there was no money at all. Just debts to leave to his wife and son. Rather sad, it was. But 'twas his own fault and no one else's. His son sent me some rather harsh letters a few years back saying that I had an obligation to him and his mother seeing as his father was my mate and had a role in helping me build up my fortune. But I was having none of that. George Windibank took his half of everything we had when we parted. If his widow was poor it was her own fault. And if the boy was poor then he could do what his father and I had done and get out and work and stop being poor and then he could look after his mother. So I gave the lad a firm rebuke and told him to be more like his father and less like his mother. I did not hear back but I am sure he did not like what I told him."

"I'm sure he did not," I ventured. "And do you have any knowledge as to what happened to young George and his mother?"

"The mother died in penury," he answered. "It was most peculiar, but young George ended up marrying my nephew's widow. Must have kept in contact somehow. I hope he's happy. She is a bit of a tough mother, she is. Doesn't give the time of day to those she thinks lazy. She'll be kicking his backside and putting him to work she will. Has no use for layabouts. No not her."

"She would have been quite a few years older than young George, would she not?" I asked. "You said that George did not have any children until much later in his life."

"Oh no," he replied and I could see a bit of a smile curling the corners of his mouth. "My nephew's widow was well into her forties. Getting close to fifty. But a healthy widow is often happy to have a much younger man around the house, or at least around the bedroom, if you know what I mean."

"Well now," I said, not wishing to pursue that line of conversation. "I hope they are getting on. And again please let me thank you on behalf of Sherlock Holmes."

"Right. Well now you tell Mr. Sherlock Holmes that I was happy to oblige. But you better make haste and get your study published Doctor Watson. I wouldn't want to get old while waiting for it."

I gave a hearty laugh and he responded in kind. I held out my hand before remembering that in his near blindness he could not see what I was doing. So I gave him a friendly clap on his boney, shrunken shoulder and bid him good day. Then I made my way as quickly as possible back to Baker Street.

I was dismayed but not surprised to hear the newspaper vendors shouting at the top of their lungs "JACK THE RIPPER STRIKES AGAIN!" The early editions of the Saturday papers were on the streets. The posters read "JACK IS BACK", "JACK GETS AHEAD" and similar sensational claims. *The Times,* to its credit ran a headline claiming only that a gruesome murder had taken place in Fenchurch. *The Star* and the other barbarians of Fleet Street all were claiming that Jack the Ripper had re-appeared. I glanced through a copy that we were handed as we crossed Piccadilly. On the interior page there was a note, buried near the end of the story, stating that Scotland Yard had claimed that there was no possibility the Jack had done the deed. But that did not stop the editors from misleading their readers and doing everything possible to panic the public and sell more newspapers.

To my frustration Holmes did not return to Baker Street until supper time, whereupon I told him all I had learned in my visit with the aged Mr. Peter Sutherland.

"What did you learn of the papers, the asset ownerships and negotiable securities he handed over to our headless imposters?" queried Holmes.

"Nothing," I responded. "My pretense was the issue of criminal justice and penal reform, not the managing of inheritances."

"All the same," rebuked Holmes, "you might have found some way to discern more. It would not have taken overly much imagination."

My short-lived pride at what I had been able to accomplish was crushed, yet again. Perhaps noticing my now sullen face Holmes added, "Ahh, but persisting in the matter of the Windibank father and son was most ingenious. Well done, Watson. Although I am not at all sure how this new data fits into our puzzle. I have no doubt that it does in some way, but all I see is a fog when I try to discern its relevance."

Having finished super, Holmes returned to his chair and lit a pipe. He said nothing. Then he let a second pipe and again said nothing. Only when the second pipe was exhausted did he turn to me and say, "I fear that tomorrow morning we will have to return to the Reform Club and meet again with Mr. Peter Sutherland. He will be horrified to learn that the people to whom he gave over several hundred thousand pounds were imposters, but we need to know as exactly as possible what was transferred. If we have that information we may, or I should say Mycroft may, be able to halt any transactions of those securities. I assume that he will show up at the Club sometime following breakfast. It will be Sunday but from what you have said, Watson, I do not assume that he would be attending church services."

"Most unlikely. I am quite sure he will be back in the club by ten o'clock."

I did not sleep well. It had been a long day that had started with the gruesome headless bodies of two young people. I could only hope and pray that the other young couple, the ones whose identities had been stolen by the deceased, would not meet the same fate.

I slept late on Sunday morning, exhausted no doubt from the long hours of the previous day. On entering our parlor I saw Sherlock Holmes already sitting and reading some documents. I did not ask but I assumed that he had not slept at all, as was the usual situation when his burning intellect and his hot determination were combined against whoever was engaging in brutal villainy.

"Any news?" I asked.

Holmes looked up and nodded. "Lestrade sent over some reports. He and his men are not complete imbeciles all of the time. They are devoid of imagination and deductive capacity but when it comes to plodding police work and the asking of endless questions they can be quite effective. He is telling me that he is close to identifying the killer of the young prop and barmaid."

"How has he managed to do that?"

"The couple was seen last in the pub where the girl had been a barmaid. She has friends there and they remembered seeing her. The two of them were chatting with some big chap who had a moustache, a red scar across his left cheek beginning in the corner of his mouth. And he spoke with a distinct Cornish accent. More questioning led to the chap's name. He calls himself Bill Sykes but I have to assume that it is a false name. Lestrade's men were able to find out where he lived – a boarding house on Hayward Street in the East End. When they arrived there was not a trace of the Cornishman but there was a mass of dried blood on the floor, and in the bins behind the house they discovered the severed heads of our unfortunate young couple who had stolen the identities of another."

"You wouldn't think that some scarred chap from Cornwall is behind this whole scheme, would you?"

"Of course not," said Holmes. "He is nothing more than a paid killer doing what he was told. No, if Mycroft is right, and I have no reason to believe he is not, this is the work of a newly formed criminal syndicate that not only commit crimes in their own interests but will undertake murders, extortion and fraud for hire for anyone willing to pay their exorbitant fee. It is all headed up by this mysterious professor that no one can ever find and who keep himself far removed from the actual criminal acts that he directs.

“His syndicate is now in the possession, we must conclude, of a very valuable bundle of securities. They will attempt to transfer these into cash as quickly but as stealthily as possible. If we can spot them doing so and follow them it should lead us back to the center of the web. For that reason we must return to the Reform Club tomorrow morning and see what we can learn from Uncle Peter about the documents he handed over.”

7 REFORM AND CLARIDGES

We departed Baker Street and as it was a clear Sunday morning walked over to Pall Mall. London on a Sunday morning in November can be a pleasant place, what with church bells peeling out hymns and Londoners dressed in their finery coming and going to religious services. We arrived at the Reform Club at an hour that we thought appropriate for finding the old man and chatting again with him. The porter smiled at us when the name of Sherlock Holmes was given and asked us to wait briefly whilst he summoned the Assistant General Secretary of the Club.

"Welcome gentlemen to the Reform Club," said the Assistant Secretary. "I had heard that you were here yesterday Dr. Watson. I am so sorry I missed you. And now you have returned and brought the famous Mr. Sherlock Holmes with you. Splendid. May I introduce you to some of our members? They are a rather adventurous lot and would love to be able to go home to their wives and boast that they had had a conversation with Sherlock Holmes."

"Thank you, but no," said Holmes, friendly but firmly. "I am working on a case that involves Mr. Peter Sutherland, and his safety and that of his family may be at risk. So if you would be so kind, do not show us around the Club. Please just arrange for a meeting with Mr. Sutherland."

"Yes, yes, indeed," said the Assistant Secretary, who had suddenly stopped beaming at Sherlock Holmes. "Perhaps you could step into my office to discuss the matter in private. Maintaining confidential mattes regarding our members is of utmost importance to the Club."

We entered his oak paneled office. It was festooned with maps and carvings and artifacts from all corners of the world, gifts to the Club from those many members who came and went to the far reaches of the Empire and beyond.

"It is very kind of you to welcome is, sir," said Holmes. "However it is rather urgent that we meet and speak with Mr. Peter Sutherland. If he is present may we speak with him? Now please sir."

The man frowned. "Certainly you could Mr. Holmes. He has been here every day for the past three weeks. But it so happens that he has not yet arrived this morning. Rather surprising as he usually shows up by half past eight. Never fails. Did not give us any notice of his plans and had registered for the luncheon. Maybe there is a problem with the old fellow. He is getting on. Over eighty I understand."

Holmes looked worried and then asked, "Has he had any unusual visitors call on him in the past two weeks?"

"Ah, yes, an interesting question. Not surprising you ask it. I thought you might, Mr. Holmes. And yes, a couple of weeks back a young couple appeared at the door. Pleasant types they were but not of the sort we normally have visit the Club. They were accompanied by an older man, exceptionally well-dressed. He did not give his name but just waited in the foyer. The young fellow, big young lad he was, gave their names to the porter and said they had an appointment to meet Mr. Sutherland and that the young woman was his great niece. They were listed in the appointment book and so we showed them in and set them up with Mr. Sutherland in one of our private rooms. I know all this because the porter came straightaway to my office and had a very puzzled look on his face. He asked if I would mind just doing a quick look in on Mr. Sutherland and his guests because he thought there was something very odd about them. So I did, just pretended that it was a normal sort of welcome-to-the-club kind of thing and I got a good look at the young man.

"Now sir we don't admit this publically, but as you are a detective then I assume you must know that our members are not like the stuffed-shirt types from the City who belong to some of the more snobbish clubs up and down Pall Mall. Our fellows are more the sporting types, travelers and all. So as you might be aware, and I sure you are, there is a fair bit of wagering goes on here especially on our sporting events."

I could not resist commenting on this and added, "Mr. Secretary, I would say it is more than a fair bit. The Reform Club is the liveliest place in London for a sporting man to place a wager. A place loved by all true sportsmen."

"Ah, thank you doctor. You are very tactful in your phrasing. Because of this activity our staff have to be up on all the leagues and games and team members. They know all the odds being offered, and give our members no end of good reliable tips for their bets. So when I looked in on Mr. Sutherland's guests I had a bit of a surprise. Now of course I did not let on but the large young man sitting there, who had given his name as Mr. Hosmer Angel, was none other than Oswald Whinery, the bull of a forward and indomitable prop of the team that just returned from overseas. Now it is not unknown for some athletes to use other names to avoid publicity, nor for our members to be met by people using false names so as to avoid possible embarrassment, but was Ozzie Whineray that notorious that he would have to be secretive? I thought not. And he has a reputation as a fine young man and there would be reason for either him or Mr. Sutherland to hide his identity. So it was very puzzling.

"When they departed, as I am told by the porter and the doorman, they were carrying a file of papers, and they entered into a very elegant carriage with the older fellow who had been waiting for them. I might have just let the whole thing go and not thought about it again, but three days ago another young man comes by and gives his name to the porter and says that he is Mr. Hosmer Angel and he registers an appointment to meet with Mr. Peter Sutherland yesterday afternoon, just a couple of hours after your meeting had ended, doctor. So as soon as he has departed the porter comes to my office and tells me that a second Mr. Angel is coming to meet Mr. Sutherland. As that was very peculiar I made a point of being at the front desk when the young fellow was expected yesterday."

"Yes, and what happened," asked Holmes.

"He never came. Mr. Sutherland kept asking if he had arrived but he never did. The old man was quite put out. He left after tea time and returned to his hotel."

"And which hotel might that be," asked Holmes.

"Claridges. But before you go running off there, as I sure you want to do, there is one other piece of information that might be of use to you."

"Please sir."

"Immediately after the visit of the first young couple, the one where I am quite sure the young man was Ozzie Whineray, Mr. Sutherland called one of our stewards and gave him an envelope and asked to have it sent to his box in Lloyds Bank. If can give me a minute I am sure we can find the details in our record book. Not that it will do you any good on a Sunday. But come Monday morning you could follow up if need be."

"That would be very helpful, sir. If you could do that, sir."

The Assistant Secretary of the Club checked the recent record book and wrote the address of the bank and the box number on a slip of paper and handed it to us.

"Mr. Holmes, I can tell by the look on your face that something quite unpleasant is taking place. We've become quite fond of old Mr. Sutherland even though we have only recently gotten to know him. If there is anything we can do, you know where to find us."

"Quite so," replied Holmes. "You have been very generous with your time and your information. We thank you sir."

Before leaving Holmes sat at a writing desk and wrote out a note. He took a stub of sealing wax, lit a match and with a signet ring sealed it. On the pavement alongside the door of the club there were three boys in page uniforms standing by their bicycles. Holmes approached the first of them and gave him the note and a shilling. The lad looked at it and his mouth opened widely. He showed the address to his fellows and they let out a whoop or two. Then he jumped on his bicycle and sped off in the direction of Westminster.

We hailed a cab. "To Claridges," shouted Holmes.

It was not far to Mayfair, and the route took us through some of the most elegant urban neighborhoods in London. By now it was past noon and the gentlefolk from Mayfair and Belgravia were out on the streets in the finest winter fashions. By the time we reached Brook Street the crowds on the pavements had vanished and we made our way into the fashionable lobby of Claridges. Holmes walked up to the young man on the front desk, most likely a member of the weekend staff, and announced his name and stated that we were here to see Mr. Peter Sutherland. The lad looked as if panic had struck. He immediately turned and entered the offices of the hotel. A minute later an older gentleman in a fine suit and trousers, and who I assumed to be the manager, emerged.

"Mr. Holmes, Dr. Watson, will you please join me in my office for just a minute."

This was the second time that day that we had been hustled off into a manager's office.

"Please gentlemen, be seated. I understand that you have asked to see our guest, Mr. Peter Sutherland, is that correct?"

"Thank you sir," said Holmes as he remained standing. "We are here to see your guest. We have already informed your man at the front desk of that fact and he has informed you. I am quite sure that you do not need to have it confirmed. Please sir, you are wasting my time and yours. Kindly have the desk call on Mr. Sutherland and inform him that we are here and need to speak to him."

"I am terribly sorry, Mr. Holmes, that will not be possible."

"Do not be ridiculous, sir," said Holmes quite sharply. "I have called on many guests at this hotel. Messages are sent immediately. There is no reason for your obstructing this visit. Please announce our visit to Mr. Sutherland."

"It will not be possible, Mr. Holmes, because Mr. Sutherland is dead."

Sherlock Holmes said nothing in reply but I watched him and saw his shoulders fall and heard a quiet sign emerge from his face.

I spoke to the manager. "My name is Doctor John Watson. We are friends of Mr. Sutherland's family. Could you kindly tell us what happened?"

"All I can say, gentlemen, is that the old man died last night in his sleep. He took his supper here last evening and entered his rooms sometime shortly after nine o'clock. He did not come down for breakfast. The housekeeping maid knocked on his room at nine o'clock this morning and there was no answer. She knocked again at ten. Then at eleven she unlocked the door and entered and found the old fellow dead in his bed. A funeral director and doctor have been sent for. I expect they will arrive very soon."

"Have you notified his next of kin," I asked.

"We had an address for his great niece but were unable to locate her. I have just received word that another niece is visiting London and staying in Camberwell and she has been sent for. And gentlemen as you are not members of the family I cannot say more nor allow you any access to see the deceased. I must bid you good-day and ask you now to leave Claridges. Thank you gentlemen and good-day." He opened his door and gestured to us to exit.

"You know who I am sir," said Holmes. "You know that I would not be here unless there were something untoward taking place. I am sure I could expedite whatever processes are required and save you a visit by a squad from Scotland Yard if you would grant us access to Mr. Sutherland's rooms."

"I am quite sure sir that you could not," answered the manager firmly. "Please gentlemen." Again he gestured for us to exit and again Sherlock Holmes did not move.

"Sir, if I may be blunt. I strongly suspect foul play in the death of your guest. To be forewarned is to be forearmed and any information I am able to secure would be fully disclosed to you."

"I am sufficiently forearmed, sir, as I know that foul play could not have taken place. Our guest was inside his room alone from the time he entered it until the time the maid found him late this morning. This hotel is secured by the most advanced locks available. They were all set at nine o'clock last night. No one passed the front desk and it would have been impossible for anyone to approach his room without our knowing. I am sorry to disappoint you, Mr. Holmes, but there is no mystery except for our doctor to discern whether the cause of death was heart failure or some other normal event that overtakes elderly people. Please gentlemen."

Standing out in the cold air on Brook Street I looked at Sherlock Holmes and noticed the signs of anger in his face. He did not take kindly to having his work obstructed, particularly when he believed that his client was in peril. Then there appeared a brief smile at the corners of his mouth.

"Come Watson," he said. "We are about to offer this excellent hotel our services, gratis."

"And what, Holmes, are you planning to do?"

"Why test their security services and give them a full report as to how they should be upgraded so that their guests may be even better served."

I followed him around to the back of the hotel. There was a door to the go-down leading into the furnace room. Holmes pulled out a small set of tools from his coat pocket and in about ten seconds picked the lock and opened the door. The furnace room door took him about five seconds.

"The servants' stairway is this way," he said walking through the basement. "Only the weekend staff are on duty. If we encounter any we will tell the truth and say we are doing a security check."

"But we have no idea what floor or what room he is in," I protested in a loud whisper.

"Of course we do. A fine hotel does not put wealthy elderly gentlemen on the higher floors. More than one flight of stairs can be a killer. He will be on the first floor, as there are no suites on the ground floor."

"But what room? There are at least forty of them. We can't go breaking into every one of them. How can you possibly know what door is his?"

Holmes gave me a quick form of The Look. First degree only thankfully.

"The cold one."

Hmm, I thought. That does make sense. The last thing a reputable hotel wants is the smell of a decomposing body in a warm room. The management would have turned down the heat and thrown open the windows, turning an elegant bedroom into a makeshift refrigerated morgue.

We met no one on the servants' staircase. As we walked quickly along the hallway of the first floor I took one side and Holmes the other and we held our hands to the keyholes. After about my tenth door I stopped and gave a low whistle to Holmes, then beckoned him to come over.

"Excellent, my dear doctor. There is a steady stream of quite cold air coming through the keyhole. Now please, allow me." Yet again it took about five seconds and Holmes turned the handle and opened the door.

We entered a large and beautifully furnished sitting room. Holmes put his hand on my arm and bade me stand still. "Give me just a few minutes to inspect. I should be much more thorough but time is being pressed."

He walked first towards the writing desk and looked it over carefully. Then he got down on his hands and knees, pulled his glass from his pocket and crawled slowly towards the bedroom. When he reached the door he stood up and waived at me to follow him.

"There is cigar ash in the ash tray. It is of a brand from a rather cheap cheroot that is seldom sold in London but quite popular in the south-west. It is certainly not available in New Zealand. The writing paper is fresh," he said, "but the ink well has been left open. The numerous marks on the carpet by the desk chair indicate that significant activity took place there, most likely a struggle. There are parallel scuff marks in lines leading from the desk all the way to the bed."

"The body was moved into the bedroom with the heels dragging," I offered. "Excellent, Watson. Now please sir, do be a doctor and take a look at the deceased."

In the bed was the body of an elderly gentleman. It had turned blue with death and the cold temperature.

"There are distinct marks on his neck. Some sort of ligature. I would have to say he has been strangled."

"Ah yes. My thoughts as well. What do you see that he is wearing?"

"His dressing gown."

"And underneath?"

"Why his evening clothes except for his suit jacket."

"And on his feet?"

I pulled back the covers. "He still has his shoes on."

"Precisely. Whoever entered this room came up quickly behind the old man, strangled him, dragged him to the bedroom and threw him in bed all in haste. So much so that he did not even take the time to remove the old man's shoes. Then he left and locked the door behind him. Not a sound was heard. A very efficient murder."

I was about to say something but stopped when I heard the door to the hallway open in the sitting room. I could hear the voice of the manger as he entered.

"This way ladies, please. I know that this is terribly distressing to you. But your uncle, madam, was an elderly gentleman and we all have to bid farewell to this life at some time. I can assure you that his last moments on this earth were a time of a delicious meal, and a warm comfortable bed. He could not have departed in a more serene way than in the comfort and security of a dinner and bedroom at Claridges. Please, the bedroom is this way and try not to be alarmed at the appearance of the body. Your uncle is now in an even more splendid place than even the finest hotel in London."

Mrs. Angel and Mrs. Windibank entered the bedroom. Holmes and I were standing on either side of the bed with the deceased between us. On seeing us they both gasped.

"Oh no."

"Oh dear."

I thought the hotel manager was about to burst in apoplexy. His face went red with anger. He strode immediately over to Sherlock Holmes and placed his face less than two inches away from the detective's.

"Get out of this hotel in an instant or I will call our security officers and they will forcibly throw you out! And if you are injured it will be on your own head."

I thought for a moment about offering a scientific opinion on the likelihood of throwing someone from the front door of a hotel and their landing on their heads but Holmes spoke before I could.

"I'm quite certain sir that with a modicum of effort you could do better than that and call Scotland Yard and inform them that one of your guests has been murdered."

Then turning to Mrs. Angel and Mrs. Windibank he said in a gracious manner, "My dear ladies I am so sorry to have to be the bearer of such tragic news. Your Uncle Peter did not pass away peaceably in his sleep last night. Someone entered his room, strangled him and placed him in bed still wearing his clothes and his shoes. The only consolation I can offer is that his death came very quickly and he was not in pain for more than a minute or two before passing out."

The manager was speechless. I walked up to him and quietly spoke close to his ear. "There are obvious marks of strangulation on his neck. Your own doctors will confirm this as will the coroner. It would be good to call Scotland Yard as quickly as possible."

He persisted. "No one could have entered his room. The doors were locked."

"Oh my," said Holmes sarcastically. "And how is it you suppose we entered. Are we fairies who flew in through the window? And if I may sir I would advise you to replace all of your locks with most recent offering from the chaps at Chubb. They are far from foolproof but vastly better than your present ones."

I then turned to the two ladies. "Ladies, this is yet another tragedy to befall you here in London. May I suggest that a cup of tea in the hotel's parlor might help to calm your spirits."

"Do they not serve brandy?"

"I could use a bit of whisky, doctor. Shouldn't they have some at a place this posh?"

Over brandy and whiskey we sat as Sherlock Holmes enlightened the mothers concerning what he had discerned so far.

"Your Uncle was an exceptionally wealthy man who knew he was not long for this earth. In order to avoid outrageous taxes, unconscionable delays, and ridiculous fees paid to solicitors he sought to transfer ownership to his beneficiaries, your children, by way of outright gift while he was yet alive. A very nasty criminal syndicate must have heard about this plan and laid a very intricate plot to intercept the documents. The foolish young couple who impersonated your children have been gruesomely murdered. All of the documents are now in the possession of the syndicate. That is all we know at this time. I can assure you that I, along with Scotland Yard and the special services of Her Majesty's government, will do everything in own power to thwart their plans and bring these monsters to justice.

"I regret that I cannot explain more at this time. And now please, ladies, if you will excuse Doctor Watson and me we must continue in our pursuit. I would not be at all surprised however that this excellent hotel would be willing to offer you a complimentary room for the remainder of your stay here in London."

"Oh my, that wouldn't that be lovely."

"Oh yes. Lovely. A shame we cannot thank Uncle Peter for making the arrangements."

A cab from Claridges took us to the front door of Lloyds Bank in the City. I had muttered something about it being impossible to gain entry on a Sunday but Holmes had just given me The Look and muttered "Mycroft" in return.

On the pavement in front of the door was a gaunt middle-aged man in a gray suit, gray hat, gray whiskers, and gray hair. He nodded at us and said only, "Holmes and Watson?"

We nodded whereupon he unlocked the door of the bank and we entered. He locked it again from the inside immediately after we had entered. Five more doors and locks were passed in the same manner until we were in a secure room where then bank served those who wished to examine the contents of their secure boxes. The gray man left us there for several minutes. Holmes and I sat in silence waiting for his return. He appeared bearing a small security box which he placed in front of us. From another pocket he withdrew yet another key an opened the box.

“Gentlemen,” he said.”You may take the contents with you or examine them here. What is your wish gentlemen?”

“We will take these with us and we thank you for your extraordinary service on a Sunday afternoon. It has been very good of you sir,” said Holmes.

“Goodness had nothing to do with it sir,” he responded. “Please follow me and I will see you back out.”

Yet another cab ride took us to Westminster. As we traveled Holmes looked through the small stack of papers that were in Mr. Sutherland’s box at Lloyds. “Ah ha!” he let out with a grim smile. “Exactly what I was hoping the old boy would have put here.”

“Come Holmes. What is it?”

“A list bearing the titles and the registered numbers of all of the securities that were given to the now departed couple. And look, he had her sign it acknowledging acceptance.”

I was looking at a page bearing a list of names and numbers. At the bottom was a brief paragraph acknowledging that the signer had received them. It was signed with the name ‘Marie Angle’.

I looked at the name and then at Holmes. He said, “It would appear that the departed Mrs. Whineray suspected something was rotten in the state of Denmark and deliberately signed with a falsified name. She is helping us from beyond the grave. I am quite sure that she must have been an excellent barmaid.”

I said nothing, pained again at the loss of a sporting young couple whose only fault had been their gullibility.

At Westminster Holmes alighted and disappeared behind a gate. Twenty minutes later he re-appeared.

"By tomorrow morning any bank or brokerage house in the nation that is capable of exchanging securities for cash will be telling their customers that due to recent problems with the telegraph system any transactions involving securities that had previously been registered in Australia or New Zealand will, with deep regret, take four days to settle. So could the customer please return on Thursday? Thank you very much. We appreciate your patience and value your business."

"Really Homes. Can Mycroft just issue such an order to every financial house in the land?"

"Of course he cannot. He never orders. He always only requests. Those houses that do not happily honor his requests will be met with a never ending line of bank inspectors, several a day, for the next year. It is always much to their benefit to honor his request, happily of course. No matter which financial house our villains present themselves to they will be met with the same story."

"But there are several hundred such houses in south England, "I protested. "Even Mycroft can't be watching all of them. How can you possibly know which ones they will come to?"

"We can't, my dear friend. We only have to know which ones they will come back to in four days. I would imagine that our master villain will not be so foolish as to try to sell all of the securities at once. He will trickle them out but his men will have to return to the first test locations on Thursday and we, or at least I should say, Mycroft's boys, with some help from Lestrade, will be there to follow them back to the center of the web."

"You are truly a genius Holmes." He smiled. He secretly enjoyed having his brilliance acknowledged. I continued. "Did you come up with this plan entirely by yourself?"

Holmes said nothing for a moment. Then, "Mycroft made some contribution." Then a moment later. "As did Lestrade." And finally, "As did Mrs. Windibank and Mrs. Angel."

"The mothers? What in heaven's name were they doing there?"

"Mycroft had sent for them. Cut short their whiskey and brandy. He had wrung more information out of them than I ever could. He is exceptionally methodical. Mrs. Windibank was the one who suggested making them wait to get their money. She suggested that we make them wait a year but Mycroft assured her that would not be realistic."

"And Mrs. Angel?"

"She agreed."

"Of course. And what will you do until Thursday?"

"Most regrettably I will not be able to lull my brain with cocaine for fear that something untoward might happen before Thursday, so I am quite certain, my good doctor, that I will go partially insane with the waiting."

I was quite certain he was right.

8 MY WRONG RIGHT

Fortunately I had the benefit of having patients waiting for me to attend to who had managed to remain healthy all weekend and then to take ill on Monday. The English are rather good at doing that. Malingering is I fear becoming a national epidemic, rearing its ugly head every Monday morning. The epidemic is unknown in Ireland. They are far more honest and just claim to be too hung over to work.

At supper time I returned to Baker Street.

"Well Holmes, any news?"

"Our little scheme is working, Watson. Two men appeared at brokerage houses in the City seeking to exchange securities for cash. Another entered a bank on Oxford Street, and another, but matching the description of one of the chaps who appeared in the City entered a small branch in Hampstead Heath just before closing hour. All were told exactly the same thing – that the telegraph system between London and the Antipodes was having some delays and could they please return on Thursday."

"And you Holmes? How goes the battle my friend?"

"Under the circumstances I am in reasonable health. I made some effort, since you had initiated the idea, of writing a monograph on the effectiveness of various forms of imprisonment and a rationale for prison reform."

"Wonderful. That should keep you busy looking for the correct answer to that problem for, I would say, about the next fifty years. Well done."

He said nothing. Tuesday was a repeat of the previous day except that six visits had been made to financial houses. Four were in the City, one in a branch just off Regent Street, and again one late in the afternoon in another small bank in Hampstead Heath. There were only three individuals involved however and Lestrade had secured detailed descriptions of all of them. One had a scar on his cheek and spoke with a Cornish accent.

"They are trying various houses," Holmes observed. "They are receiving the same consistent response. There is no reason for them to suspect that we are on to them."

Wednesday was the same. Four new houses were visited and a larger institution in the City that was visited on Monday had a repeat visit. There was no attempt in Hampstead Heath. I thought it unlikely that there would be more than two bank branches in that small village that would deal with securities and I assumed our villains have come to the same conclusion.

I arrived back at Baker Street early on Thursday afternoon, all eager to hear if the plan was working.

"Have we found our blackguards?" I shouted as I quickly climbed the stairs.

There was no answer. I entered and found Holmes quietly smoking on his pipe.

"Holmes. An answer. Out with it."

"There was no action at all today. No one visited a brokerage and no one came to collect," he replied calmly.

I was alarmed. "What is the meaning? Have they seen through us? Will they run off to America and try to cash the certificates there? Is all lost?"

"Oh, my dear doctor," he responded. "Not at all. No, not at all. It is only undeniable proof that we are dealing with a serious and professional criminal. Haste and greed are the downfall of the lower criminal classes. Whoever is behind this scheme is content to wait a day, perhaps a week or more. He knows that his funds will eventually be in his hands and that anything that is precipitous would create suspicion. And I confess, my dear Watson, I trust you will not think it vain of me, but I am secretly rather pleased that a new and professional class of criminal has emerged in London. I was getting frightfully bored of the commonplace, especially since we did away with Mr. Ripper."

I did think it a little vain of Holmes but was relieved to know that if indeed a new professional level of criminality was about to spread like a disease through London that it would be met by the scourge of justice administered by Sherlock Holmes. As to Jack, I knew better than to ask.

"So what do we do now?"

"We wait until tomorrow. And tomorrow. And tomorrow."

"Holmes. Stop it. If I wish to hear Macbeth whining I am sure I could go to the Lyceum for a better rendition."

"Ah, well then, if you will not appreciate my drama I trust you will my musicianship." He picked up his violin and began to play a short piece of his own composing. I would have to wait until tomorrow.

I did not inform Holmes but I sent word to my medical office that all appointments for the day were to be cancelled and put over until Monday. The English generally do not take ill on Friday afternoon. I waited in Baker Street with Holmes. He pretending to work on his monograph and I reading the latest *Lancet.*

At three o'clock there was a polite knock on the door. Mrs. Hudson opened it and with a sideways look at first Holmes then me said, "Constable Mactavish to see you." I knew that the dear lady was not in the least surprised and only dying of curiosity.

"My dear Mrs. Hudson," I assured here. "If all goes well you will learn all about it in *The Strand.* Mind you it might not appear there for a year, but just be patient." She gave me a glare and I am quite sure that were I within arm's reach I might had had a pinch on the cheek and accused of being saucy.

The constable was all business. "Mr. Holmes and Doctor Watson, could you please come with me now. We have a carriage waiting around the corner." Holmes gave me a questioning look and held his hand with his finger pointing like a gun. I nodded and patted the pocket of my jacket. He in turn patted the pocket of his and I nodded in return.

Holmes, the constable and I climbed into a closed four-seater, drawn by a brace of powerful horses. There was another man seated already. He put his head out the window and spoke to the driver. "Hampstead Heath. Back door of the inn."

I recognized the chap as an inspector from Scotland Yard but could not remember his name. We bounced along Marleybone Road for several blocks, making slow progress in the busy Friday afternoon. No one spoke. After we had turned left on Eversholt and cleared some of the mayhem of London the constable leaned over to the inspector and I heard him say, "What is the reason for sending in the Royal Marines. We have enough boys to handle it without them."

Without turning to answer him the inspector quietly replied, "Lestrade arranged it. Says there could be some fireworks and better the marines taking it than us. They're paid for combat."

"Hmm," said the constable and that was the end of the conversation. As we started to climb Haverstock Hill the inspector chap reached into his pocket and handed over a sealed letter to Holmes. "You appear to have some important friends, sir," he said. I could just make out the seal and knew that it came from somewhere deep within Westminster.

Holmes read the letter slowly, finishing it just before we reached the village adjacent to Hampstead Heath. "We are to wait at the inn. There will be no action until midnight. They have traced three men who tried to cash the certificates to a small estate house just outside the village. It is believed that my clients are inside. However we have no way of knowing how many men our enemy has beyond the three. Lestrade has a dozen of his boys and Mycroft has sent as many marines. They are taking this affair very seriously, I must say."

We entered the inn, arranged for a room for the night, and sat in the dining area and ordered a brandy, but only one each. There were a score of other guests and the conversation was lively as is common on a Friday afternoon once folks are done work for the week.

"Do you observe that fellow by the window?" asked Holmes nodding towards the far wall.

"With the tweed jacket and cap. Yes what about him? He looks a little distressed."

"Very. Can you discern who he is?"

I looked intently at the man. He was of average height and weight and around thirty years of age I guessed. He was quite fidgety and read and re-read a note in his hands, and kept looking towards the entrance of the room.

"Beyond that he is disconcerted and expecting someone, no I cannot see anything else that could help me say who he is. Surely you cannot, Holmes."

"He is George Windibank the younger."

"Holmes, how can you possibly know that? There are hundreds, thousands of possible upset young men in London on a Friday afternoon. He could be anyone of them. How could you possibly know who he is?"

"You are assuming that I am looking only at his appearance and his actions and that I have made my deduction accordingly, Watson. I would dearly love for you to believe that but the truth is I saw the name in the hotel register, and from my vantage point I can see, although you cannot, our two dear mothers standing outside the inn and about to make their entrance. I suggest that we remove ourselves before they arrive and retreat to our room."

I had no idea what Holmes was up to and utterly confused by the arrival of Mrs. Angel and Mrs. Windibank at Hampstead heath. I had thought that this situation was a closely guarded secret. Nonetheless I followed Holmes up to our rooms.

"The presence of Mr. Windibank," Holmes said, "ties some of the loose threads of this case together."

He wrote out a note using printed letters instead of cursive writing. It ran:

> Come immediately to Room 16. Final negotiations for the return of the youngsters. The door will be open.

He rang the bell for a page and gave it to him with instructions to have it delivered forthwith to Mr. George Windibank, who might be sitting with two ladies in the dining room.

Soon I heard rapid footsteps in the hall. Our door opened and an anguished voice spoke. "There is no more to give you. What sort of fiend are you?"

The voice went silent as the young man from the dining room entered. He regarded Sherlock Holmes and me and a look of shock swept over his face. He turned as if to flee but Holmes spoke loudly.

"George Windibank, regardless what role you have played in this terrible affair we are here to help save the lives of Mary and Hosmer."

The man stopped and looked at us. Fear was written across his countenance.

"Please Mr. Windibank, be seated," said Holmes. "My name is Sherlock Holmes. Your wife has told you that I have taken on this case. We are here along with several armed men and we will rescue the children if you will cooperate with us."

The chap sat in the chair, trembling. Holmes spoke to him, slowly but firmly.

"Your role in this affair has been shameful. You were very angry were you not, Mr. Windibank, that your father's mate became one of the wealthiest men in the Empire while your family lived with nothing? Your mother still lives in penury. Is that not correct? Please answer me sir."

There was no response. He was obviously bewildered, but nodded.

"You married Mrs. Windibank when she became a widow even though she was twenty years your senior in order to reclaim what you believed was rightfully yours. Is that not correct?"

Another nod, his eyes wide with fear.

"And then to your dismay and anger you found out that none of Peter Sutherland's fortune would come to your wife but would pass directly to her daughter. Again you would not see a farthing of it. Is not correct as well?

Another nod.

"But then you heard of some sort of shadowy criminal group who could make arrangements, who could fix things up, for a fee of course, and you met with them. How much did they say they would charge you?"

"One third," came the whispered reply. "And only if they succeeded."

"And you found that you had made a Faustian deal with the devil, did you not."

"I never imagined, you have to believe me sir, I never imagined that he would do what he did."

"The scheme seemed harmless enough did it not? Send the young couple on separate voyages. Have another couple pretend to be them and deceive the blind old man. Take the certificates, cash them in and split the proceeds. Again sir, am I correct?"

He looked up and took a deep breath. "Yes Mr. Holmes. You are."

"But then he changed his terms. He now wanted fifty percent. More?"

"Seventy-five."

"And did you threaten to go to the police?" asked Holmes.

"I did. And he told me to watch the papers and see what happens to people who go to the police."

"He cut their heads off," said Holmes. "And he kidnapped Mary and Hosmer and threatened to do the same to them."

Again a nod. "I could not believe that I was dealing with such a monster. He kept increasing the terms. He said he would simply take it all. I said there was no possibility of that. He could kill me first. But he killed the old man. He said that he would now kill not only Mary and Hosmer but their mothers. He told me to imagine all of them with their heads cut off. You cannot believe, sir, what this man is. He is the devil himself. He laughed when he described what had been done to Ozzie and his wife. He laughed. I have destroyed everything. I have brought the devil into our lives. You must believe that I never knew, could never have known what would happen."

The man was shaking with sobs. His head was buried in his hands. Holmes let him sob away for a few minutes and then spoke firmly.

"Mr. George Windibank you have been a foolish and greedy man and you are paying a terrible price for it. You can help us bring justice and save the lives of the young couple."

"How sir? Please. If I can do anything, sir I will."

"How came Mrs. Windibank and Mrs. Angel to this place?" asked Holmes.

"I sent them a note saying that I was trying to rescue Mary and Hosmer. I was not thinking and used the inn's stationary. They saw where it had come from and straightaway came here."

"Trying to play the hero and just continuing to deceive," said Holmes

"Yes, sir."

"Very well. The first thing you must do is go to your wife and Mrs. Angel and make a full confession. If they ever speak to you again I will be surprised. You deserve nothing else."

He nodded. "I will do that. Yes."

"And then do not leave this building. Within the hour there will be a contingent of marines and men from Scotland Yard who will storm the house. You do know which house I am referring to, do you not?"

"Yes sir."

Have you been in inside it?"

"Yes sir."

"Excellent. Then you will tell everything you can remember about the layout of the house, the out buildings, the gardens and the pathways to the officers. Your information will be quite useful."

He nodded again. "They are armed. They will kill."

"We are fully aware of the danger. The police and the marines are also armed and prepared to kill."

"He will kill Hosmer and Mary just out of spite."

"Then you will have to provide such complete information as you are able so that our fellows will make no mistake and not give them that opportunity. Now please sir, be on your way. Your wife is waiting for you."

He rose and walked slowly out of the room. He looked as if he wanted to die.

9 THE FINAL ACT

We had dinner sent up to our room. Two hours later a note arrived.

"Come Watson, the final act is about to begin."

As instructed, we moved quietly to a small barn behind the inn. In the dim light I could make out Mycroft Holmes, Inspector Lestrade and a large man in a marine uniform bearing the rank of captain. I could not see into the darkness at the back of the barn but I could hear the shuffling and breathing of what I thought must be at least twenty more men. All conversation was in whispers. It was cold. Winter had set in and all of us could see our breath as we exhaled.

"Your Mr. Windibank was very useful," said Lestrade. "We have a good idea of the house and a plan to take it by storm. If we can get close before they see us we should catch them off guard and be able to subdue them without taking any casualties ourselves. It appears the young couple are being held in a locked room in the basement. It may be a bit of a sticky wicket getting down there before the guards do. But if we move quickly we think we can do it. We move in one hour. We will wait until the lamps are all turned out for the night."

It was a very long hour. Then the marine captain gave a signal and I watched as twenty-four armed marines and police officers filed past me and walked silently up the small road that led away from the village and towards the wooded area of Hampstead Heath. Holmes and I fell in behind them. We arrived at a laneway but did not carry on down it.

"Men," we heard the marine captain say quietly. "You all know your paths to the house. Take them and wait out of sight until you have the signal and then move very quickly. If you get shot it was because you were too slow."

There were a few quiet chuckles in the ranks.

"Snipers, stay behind with me."

The soldiers and police officers moved away in the dark. Holmes, Mycroft and I followed the captain to a vantage point in the woods at the edge of the great lawn in front of the house. The lamps in the bedrooms and the parlor had all been put out. Some remained lit in the hallway and gave a dim light through the windows at the front of the house. The captain waited a full fifteen minutes and then gave the first of a series of bird calls. Each time an identical call answered. After hearing six such calls and responses, the captain turned to Mycroft and said, "Everyone is place sir. We're ready to charge."

"You are in charge Captain," said Mycroft quietly. "The battle is in yours hands."

"It's what we live to do sir," came the reply.

The captain took a long last look over the house and the grounds surrounding it and then gave a powerful blast on his whistle. I watched as nine marines all carrying rifles with bayonets mounted went running like they were on a hundred yard dash towards the house. Although cold there was no snow on the ground and they moved rapidly over the frozen ground. Three of them carried a heavy pole and when they reached the door they smashed it in a short order. Two others smashed the bay windows and disappeared inside. The police officers followed them. Other disappeared around behind the back of the house. I heard first one explosion and then another as grenades were tossed into the bedrooms. Then I heard gunfire. The rifles were making their sharp cracking sounds, followed by the loud popping bangs of revolvers. I could distinguish the sound of the police and military issue pistols, but then heard the return fire of a variety of other guns that were, I assumed, in the hands of the enemy.

It had been a long time, nearly two decades since I had served in Afghanistan and watched as brave men rushed into battle. Even though I was in the medical corps I was often at the front, bringing emergency help to the wounded. There is no such feeling on earth that compares to the intensity of battle. Once again I felt it, regretting only that I was not twenty years younger.

Soon we began to see a series of flashes. Several of the police officers had electric torches with them and were flashing them back, sending messages in code.

"Ground floor is cleared," said the captain.

"They have more men there than we expected. Three of the enemy are down. Two have surrendered. Upper floor still fighting."

There was more gunfire, and three more grenade blasts. Then more signals.

"Upper floor secured," said the captain. "Just the basement to go."

Then another series of signals.

The captain turned to me and in an urgent voice said, "Doctor. You have battlefield experience. One of our boys has been hit. It's rather bad. They're bringing him out. We have a medic on the team. Can you give him some help? He's around the back of the house."

It has been a long time since I had been placed in this position. I leapt out of the woods and ran as fast as I could towards the house and around to the back. My leg, so badly damaged twenty years ago by the Jezreel bullet from the Afghan sniper was screaming in pain but the adrenaline was pumping and I arrived at the back of the house where a young marine lay on the ground. He had taken one in the shoulder but he was not in peril. The medic handed me a pack of bandages and I went to work.

The gunfire continued inside the house and then it all went silent. Lestrade emerged from the back door. "We've got all that were fighting us. But we can't find the young couple," he said breathlessly.

In the lull we helped the wounded marine back to the protection of the wooded area where his captain, Holmes, and Mycroft were waiting.

The captain bent over his wounded man. "Next time, Jenson, remember to duck."

"Yes sir. Will do sir."

Sherlock Holmes placed his hand on the captain's shoulder and leaned over. "Captain. Coming from the shed on the far side. Please sir."

I looked over and could see two men, each of them with his arm around the neck of one of the young couple. They were walking with their heads pushed up against the faces of their hostages. One forearm was around the neck. The other arm held a revolver pointed against the temple of the one being held.

We heard a shout.

"Stand down. Back off. Or we will kill them. Drop your weapons. Drop them"

The police officers and marines who had emerged from the house all lowered their weapons. They did not drop them.

"Snipers," I heard the captain speak quietly. "At the ready."

Three marines who had been standing behind us in the woods all along came forward, dropped to one knee and raised their rifles. The captain joined them.

In a quiet voice I heard him. "Marine one, you have fellow with the gent."

"Aye sir"

"Marine two. Same thing."

"Aye sir."

"Marine three, the fellow with the girl"

"Aye sir."

"Good. I have him as well. Now on my count, on three."

I grabbed the arm of Sherlock Holmes. Mary and Hosmer were at least fifty yards away. A miss of only three inches would put a bullet in their heads. I could feel Holmes hand grasp my side. He was holding tightly to me in return.

"One. Two. Three."

Four rifles fired simultaneously. The two men who had the guns to the heads of their hostages fell backwards and it looked as if their heads had exploded.

Mycroft Holmes turned to me and his brother. "They don't miss." He turned back away from us.

No sooner had the marine snipers fired off their deadly rounds but all four of them went rushing up to the young man and women. One of them grabbed Mary around her waist from behind and using his body as a shield carried her, running towards us. A second moved quickly behind Hosmer and likewise using his body as a shield pushed the lad towards us. The other two dropped again to their knee and aimed their rifles at the direction from which the hostages had appeared.

There were no more shots. The battle was over.

In our little wooded shelter Hosmer and Mary Angel tightly embraced each other. The girl was trembling and sobbing. Over her husband's shoulder she looked a saw both Homes and I. She stopped crying and for a second made no sound. Then, "Hello Doctor Watson, Mr. Sherlock Holmes. Please tell me that this case is finally over."

Holmes and I both nodded and smiled. Mycroft simply harrumphed and walked away and conferred with Lestrade and the captain.

"The older one. Any sign of him?"

"None," answered the captain. "Searched everywhere. He got clean away. Not a sign."

"Very well, Captain. We'll try again next time."

"Next time sir?"

"Next time."

In the small hours of the morning we made our way back to Baker Street and fell exhausted into our beds and slept until late Saturday morning. A note had arrived in an envelope bearing the address of Claridges and containing an invitation to lunch.

We dressed and made our way over to Mayfair. Assembled at the luncheon table and waiting for us were Mrs. Windibank and Mrs. Angel as well as Mary and Hosmer Angel. Mary was wearing a hat, a large hat. I thought she looked quite fetching regardless of whatever opinion Sherlock Holmes had of the girl.

One of the mothers spoke. "Quite the lovely place you arranged for us to stay, Mr. Holmes."

"Really. Quite on the posh side. Just lovely."

"And we have the honeymoon suite," chimed Mary Angel.

Word had gotten to Claridges that not only had they been the site of the demise of one of the wealthiest men in the Empire, but that his grand-niece and sole heir was needing a place to stay after a trying experience. They were only too happy to oblige.

"What dear old Uncle Peter had dreaded has come to pass."

"Exactly what the old boy did not want to happen has."

"The estate will go into probate. There will be months, years of arguments in the courts."

"Those lawyers will be fighting forever over it."

"Young Mary and Hosmer will just have to keep on working and earning an honest living for a good while yet."

"Won't hurt them. Having to work for a few more years will be good for them."

"Builds character."

"They'll be better for it."

"Ladies, please," interrupted Holmes. "I am sure that the earnest men over in Chancery Lane will do their best to expedite what is sure to be a very complicated estate. It will take some time for the certificates to be cancelled and re-issued, but I would suspect that some of the funds will come through at just about the time our young couple here gets over their desire to go gadding about the globe and settle down and start a family."

"Well that could be. There is always an early risk you know. If you know what I mean."

"Yes a risk that the family could arrive early, if you know what I mean."

"Yes," continued Holmes, "but at least you, Mrs. Windibank will be freed of the free-loading of your husband."

"Oh no. I'm going to keep him around."

"She's not getting rid of him. No sir."

Here I had to speak in disbelief. "You cannot be serious, Mrs. Windibank. After everything he did and all the mayhem he caused? After his stupidity and blundering? You will still keep him?"

"He can't possibly do any harm now, and I didn't marry him for his brilliant mind, doctor."

"She didn't marry him for his conversation and companionship either, doctor. And he's harmless now"

"Then why did you?" I asked in utter bewilderment.

Both of them gave me The Look. Third degree.

"Why does any widow who has turned fifty want to marry a man twenty years her junior doctor? Must I spell it out?"

"I must find me one of them as well. A nice stalwart younger man. Just what the doctor ordered, or he should have."

"To be blunt doctor, he was rather good in his husbandly duties, if you know what I mean."

"That is what they are good for, doctor, if you know what I mean."

APPENDIX

A CASE OF IDENTITY

The original Sherlock Homes story

by

Arthur Conan Doyle

A Case of Identity

"My dear fellow," said Sherlock Holmes, as we sat on either side of the fire in his lodgings at Baker Street, "life is infinitely stranger than anything which the mind of man can invent. We would not dare to conceive the things which are really mere commonplaces of existence. If we could fly out of that window hand in hand, hover over this great city, gently remove the roofs, and peep in at the queer things which are going on, the strange coincidences, the plannings, the cross-purposes, the wonderful chains of events, working through generations, and leading to the most outre results, it would make all fiction, with its conventionalities and foreseen conclusions, most stale and unprofitable."

"And yet I am not convinced of it," I answered. "The cases which come to light in the papers are, as a rule, bald enough, and vulgar enough. We have in our police reports realism pushed to its extreme limits, and yet the result is, it must be confessed, neither fascinating nor artistic."

"A certain selection and discretion must be used in producing a realistic effect," remarked Holmes. "This is wanting in the police report, where more stress is laid perhaps upon the platitudes of the magistrate than upon the details, which to an observer contain the vital essence of the whole matter. Depend upon it, there is nothing so unnatural as the commonplace."

I smiled and shook my head. "I can quite understand your thinking so," I said. "Of course, in your position of unofficial adviser and helper to everybody who is absolutely puzzled, throughout three continents, you are brought in contact with all that is strange and bizarre. But here," - I picked up the morning paper from the ground - "let us put it to a practical test. Here is the first heading upon which I come. 'A husband's cruelty to his wife.' There is half a column of print, but I know without reading it that it is all perfectly familiar to me. There is, of course, the other woman, the drink, the push, the blow, the bruise, the unsympathetic sister or landlady. The crudest of writers could invent nothing more crude."

"Indeed your example is an unfortunate one for your argument," said Holmes, taking the paper, and glancing his eye down it. "This is the Dundas separation case, and, as it happens, I was engaged in clearing up some small points in connection with it. The husband was a teetotaler, there was no other woman, and the conduct complained of was that he had drifted into the habit of winding up every meal by taking out his false teeth and hurling them at his wife, which you will allow is not an action likely to occur to the imagination of the average story teller. Take a pinch of snuff, doctor, and acknowledge that I have scored over you in your example."

He held out his snuffbox of old gold, with a great amethyst in the center of the lid. Its splendor was in such contrast to his homely ways and simple life that I could not help commenting upon it.

"Ah!" said he, "I forgot that I had not seen you for some weeks. It is a little souvenir from the King of Bohemia, in return for my assistance in the case of the Irene Adler papers."

"And the ring?" I asked, glancing at a remarkable brilliant which sparkled upon his finger.

"It was from the reigning family of Holland, though the matter in which I served them was of such delicacy that I cannot confide it even to you, who have been good enough to chronicle one or two of my little problems."

"And have you any on hand just now?" I asked with interest.

"Some ten or twelve, but none which present any features of interest. They are important, you understand, without being interesting. Indeed I have found that it is usually in unimportant matters that there is a field for the observation, and for the quick analysis of cause and effect which gives the charm to an investigation. The larger crimes are apt to be the simpler, for the bigger the crime, the more obvious, as a rule, is the motive. In these cases, save for one rather intricate matter which has been referred to me from Marseilles, there is nothing which presents any features of interest. It is possible, however, that I may have something better before very many minutes are over, for this is one of my clients, or I am much mistaken."

He had risen from his chair, and was standing between the parted blinds, gazing down into the dull, neutral-tinted London street. Looking over his shoulder, I saw that on the pavement opposite there stood a large woman with a heavy fur boa round her neck, and a large curling red feather in a broad-brimmed hat which was tilted in a coquettish Duchess-of-Devonshire fashion over her ear.

From under this great panoply she peeped up in a nervous, hesitating fashion at our windows, while her body oscillated backward and forward, and her fingers fidgeted with her glove buttons. Suddenly, with a plunge, as of the swimmer who leaves the bank, she hurried across the road, and we heard the sharp clang of the bell.

"I have seen those symptoms before," said Holmes, throwing his cigarette into the fire. "Oscillation upon the pavement always means an affaire de coeur. She would like advice, but is not sure that the matter is not too delicate for communication. And yet even here we may discriminate. When a woman has been seriously wronged by a man, she no longer oscillates, and the usual symptom is a broken bell wire. Here we may take it that there is a love matter, but that the maiden is not so much angry as perplexed or grieved. But here she comes in person to resolve our doubts."

As he spoke, there was a tap at the door, and the boy in buttons entered to announce Miss Mary Sutherland, while the lady herself loomed behind his small black figure like a full-sailed merchantman behind a tiny pilot boat. Sherlock Holmes welcomed her with the easy courtesy for which he was remarkable, and having closed the door, and bowed her into an armchair, he looked her over in the minute and yet abstracted fashion which was peculiar to him.

"Do you not find," he said, "that with your short sight it is a little trying to do so much typewriting?"

"I did at first," she answered, "but now I know where the letters are without looking." Then, suddenly realizing the full purport of his words, she gave a violent start, and looked up with fear and astonishment upon her broad, good-humored face. "You've heard about me, Mr. Holmes," she cried, "else how could you know all that?"

"Never mind," said Holmes, laughing, "it is my business to know things. Perhaps I have trained myself to see what others overlook. If not, why should you come to consult me?"

"I came to you, sir, because I heard of you from Mrs. Etherege, whose husband you found so easily when the police and everyone had given him up for dead. Oh, Mr. Holmes, I wish you would do as much for me. I'm not rich, but still I have a hundred a year in my own right, besides the little that I make by the machine, and I would give it all to know what has become of Mr. Hosmer Angel."

"Why did you come away to consult me in such a hurry?" asked Sherlock Holmes, with his finger tips together, and his eyes to the ceiling.

Again a startled look came over the somewhat vacuous face of Miss Mary Sutherland. "Yes, I did bang out of the house," she said, "for it made me angry to see the easy way in which Mr. Windibank - that is, my father - took it all. He would not go to the police, and he would not go to you, and so at last, as he would do nothing, and kept on saying that there was no harm done, it made me mad, and I just on with my things and came right away to you."

"Your father?" said Holmes. "Your stepfather, surely, since the name is different."

"Yes, my stepfather. I call him father, though it sounds funny, too, for he is only five years and two months older than myself."

"And your mother is alive?"

"Oh, yes; mother is alive and well. I wasn't best pleased, Mr. Holmes, when she married again so soon after father's death, and a man who was nearly fifteen years younger than herself. Father was a plumber in the Tottenham Court Road, and he left a tidy business behind him, which mother carried on with Mr. Hardy, the foreman; but when Mr. Windibank came he made her sell the business, for he was very superior, being a traveler in wines. They got four thousand seven hundred for the good-will and interest, which wasn't near as much as father could have got if he had been alive."

I had expected to see Sherlock Holmes impatient under this rambling and inconsequential narrative, but, on the contrary, he had listened with the greatest concentration of attention.

"Your own little income," he asked, "does it come out of the business?"

"Oh, no, sir. It is quite separate, and was left me by my Uncle Ned in Auckland. It is in New Zealand stock, paying four and half per cent. Two thousand five hundred pounds was the amount, but I can only touch the interest."

"You interest me extremely," said Holmes. "And since you draw so large a sum as a hundred a year, with what you earn into the bargain, you no doubt travel a little, and indulge yourself in every way. I believe that a single lady can get on very nicely upon an income of about sixty pounds."

"I could do with much less than that, Mr. Holmes, but you understand that as long as I live at home I don't wish to be a burden to them, and so they have the use of the money just while I am staying with them. Of course that is only just for the time. Mr. Windibank draws my interest every quarter, and pays it over to mother, and I find that I can do pretty well with what I earn at typewriting. It brings me twopence a sheet, and I can often do from fifteen to twenty sheets in a day."

"You have made your position very clear to me," said Holmes. "This is my friend, Doctor Watson, before whom you can speak as freely as before myself. Kindly tell us now all about your connection with Mr. Hosmer Angel."

A flush stole over Miss Sutherland's face, and she picked nervously at the fringe of her jacket. "I met him first at the gasfitters' ball," she said. "They used to send father tickets when he was alive, and then afterwards they remembered us, and sent them to mother. Mr. Windibank did not wish us to go. He never did wish us to go anywhere. He would get quite mad if I wanted so much as to join a Sunday School treat. But this time I was set on going, and I would go, for what right had he to prevent? He said the folk were not fit for us to know, when all father's friends were to be there. And he said that I had nothing fit to wear, when I had my purple plush that I had never so much as taken out of the drawer. At last, when nothing else would do, he went off to France upon the business of the firm; but we went, mother and I, with Mr. Hardy, who used to be our foreman, and it was there I met Mr. Hosmer Angel."

"I suppose," said Holmes, "that when Mr. Windibank came back from France, he was very annoyed at your having gone to the ball?"

"Oh, well, he was very good about it. He laughed, I remember, and shrugged his shoulders, and said there was no use denying anything to a woman, for she would have her way."

"I see. Then at the gasfitters' ball you met, as I understand, a gentleman called Mr. Hosmer Angel?"

"Yes, sir. I met him that night, and he called next day to ask if we had got home all safe, and after that we met him - that is to say, Mr. Holmes, I met him twice for walks, but after that father came back again, and Mr. Hosmer Angel could not come to the house any more."

"No?"

"Well, you know, father didn't like anything of the sort. He wouldn't have any visitors if he could help it, and he used to say that a woman should be happy in her own family circle. But then, as I used to say to mother, a woman wants her own circle to begin with, and I had not got mine yet."

"But how about Mr. Hosmer Angel? Did he make no attempt to see you?"

"Well, father was going off to France again in a week, and Hosmer wrote and said that it would be safer and better not to see each other until he had gone. We could write in the meantime, and he used to write every day. I took the letters in the morning, so there was no need for father to know."

"Were you engaged to the gentleman at this time?"

"Oh, yes, Mr. Holmes. We were engaged after the first walk that we took. Hosmer - Mr. Angel - was a cashier in an office in Leadenhall Street - and--"

"What office?"

"That's the worst of it, Mr. Holmes; I don't know."

"Where did he live, then?"

"He slept on the premises."

"And you don't know his address?"

"No - except that it was Leadenhall Street."

"Where did you address your letters, then?"

"To the Leadenhall Street Post Office, to be left till called for. He said that if they were sent to the office he would be chaffed by all the other clerks about having letters from a lady, so I offered to typewrite them, like he did his, but he wouldn't have that, for he said that when I wrote them they seemed to come from me, but when they were typewritten he always felt that the machine had come between us.

That will just show you how fond he was of me, Mr. Holmes, and the little things that he would think of."

"It was most suggestive," said Holmes. "It has long been an axiom of mine that the little things are infinitely the most important. Can you remember any other little things about Mr. Hosmer Angel?"

"He was a very shy man, Mr. Holmes. He would rather walk with me in the evening than in the daylight, for he said that he hated to be conspicuous. Very retiring and gentlemanly he was. Even his voice was gentle. He'd had the quinsy and swollen glands when he was young, he told me, and it had left him with a weak throat and a hesitating, whispering fashion of speech. He was always well dressed, very neat and plain, but his eyes were weak, just as mine are, and he wore tinted glasses against the glare."

"Well, and what happened when Mr. Windibank, your stepfather, returned to France?"

"Mr. Hosmer Angel came to the house again, and proposed that we should marry before father came back. He was in dreadful earnest, and made me swear, with my hands on the Testament, that whatever happened I would always be true to him. Mother said he was quite right to make me swear, and that it was a sign of his passion. Mother was all in his favor from the first, and was even fonder of him than I was. Then, when they talked of marrying within the week, I began to ask about father; but they both said never to mind about father, but just to tell him afterwards and mother said she would make it all right with him. I didn't quite like that, Mr. Holmes. It seemed funny that I should ask his leave, as he was only a few years older than me; but I didn't want to do anything on the sly, so I wrote to father at Bordeaux, where the company has its French offices, but the letter came back to me on the very morning of the wedding."

"It missed him, then?"

"Yes, sir, for he had started to England just before it arrived."

"Ha! that was unfortunate. Your wedding was arranged, then, for the Friday. Was it to be in church?"

"Yes, sir, but very quietly. It was to be at St. Saviour's, near King's Cross, and we were to have breakfast afterwards at the St. Pancras Hotel. Hosmer came for us in a hansom, but as there were two of us, he put us both into it, and stepped himself into a four- wheeler, which happened to be the only other cab in the street. We got to the church first, and when the four-wheeler drove up we waited for him to step out, but he never did, and when the cabman got down from the box and looked, there was no one there! The cabman said that he could not imagine what had become of him, for he had seen him get in with his own eyes. That was last Friday, Mr. Holmes, and I have never seen or heard anything since then to throw any light upon what became of him."

"It seems to me that you have been very shamefully treated," said Holmes.

"Oh, no, sir! He was too good and kind to leave me so. Why, all the morning he was saying to me that, whatever happened, I was to be true; and that even if something quite unforeseen occurred to separate us, I was always to remember that I was pledged to him, and that he would claim his pledge sooner or later. It seemed strange talk for a wedding morning, but what has happened since gives a meaning to it."

"Most certainly it does. Your own opinion is, then, that some unforeseen catastrophe has occurred to him?"

"Yes, sir. I believe that he foresaw some danger, or else he would not have talked so. And then I think that what he foresaw happened."

"But you have no notion as to what it could have been?"

"None."

"One more question. How did your mother take the matter?"

"She was angry, and said that I was never to speak of the matter again."

"And your father? Did you tell him?"

"Yes, and he seemed to think, with me, that something had happened, and that I should hear of Hosmer again. As he said, what interest could anyone have in bringing me to the door of the church, and then leaving me? Now, if he had borrowed my money, or if he had married me and got my money settled on him, there might be some reason; but Hosmer was very independent about money, and never would look at a shilling of mine. And yet what could have happened? And why could he not write? Oh! it drives me half mad to think of, and I can't sleep a wink at night." She pulled a little handkerchief out of her muff, and began to sob heavily into it.

"I shall glance into the case for you," said Holmes, rising, "and I have no doubt that we shall reach some definite result. Let the weight of the matter rest upon me now, and do not let your mind dwell upon it further. Above all, try to let Mr. Hosmer Angel vanish from your memory, as he has done from your life."

"Then you don't think I'll see him again?"

"I fear not."

"Then what has happened to him?"

"You will leave that question in my hands. I should like an accurate description of him, and any letters of his which you can spare."

"I advertised for him in last Saturday's Chronicle," said she. "Here is the slip, and here are four letters from him."

"Thank you. And your address?"

"No. 31 Lyon Place, Camberwell."

"Mr. Angel's address you never had, I understand. Where is your father's place of business?"

"He travels for Westhouse and Marbank, the great claret importers of Fenchurch Street."

"Thank you. You have made your statement very clearly. You will leave the papers here, and remember the advice which I have given you. Let the whole incident be a sealed book, and do not allow it to affect your life."

"You are very kind, Mr. Holmes, but I cannot do that. I shall be true to Hosmer. He shall find me ready when he comes back."

For all the preposterous hat and the vacuous face, there was something noble in the simple faith of our visitor which compelled our respect. She laid her little bundle of papers upon the table, and went her way, with a promise to come again whenever she might be summoned.

Sherlock Holmes sat silent for a few minutes with his finger tips still pressed together, his legs stretched out in front of him, and his gaze directed upward to the ceiling. Then he took down from the rack the old and oily clay pipe, which was to him as a counselor, and, having lighted it, he leaned back in his chair, with thick blue cloud wreaths spinning up from him, and a look of infinite languor in his face.

"Quite an interesting study, that maiden," he observed. "I found her more interesting than her little problem, which, by the way, is rather a trite one. You will find parallel cases, if you consult my index, in Andover in '77, and there was something of the sort at The Hague last year. Old as is the idea, however, there were one or two details which were new to me. But the maiden herself was most instructive."

"You appeared to read a good deal upon her which was quite invisible to me," I remarked.

"Not invisible, but unnoticed, Watson. You did not know where to look, and so you missed all that was important. I can never bring you to realize the importance of sleeves, the suggestiveness of thumb nails, or the great issues that may hang from a boot lace. Now, what did you gather from that woman's appearance? Describe it."

"Well, she had a slate-colored, broad-brimmed straw hat, with a feather of a brickish red. Her jacket was black, with black beads sewed upon it and a fringe of little black jet ornaments. Her dress was brown, rather darker than coffee color, with a little purple plush at the neck and sleeves. Her gloves were grayish, and were worn through at the right forefinger. Her boots I didn't observe. She had small round, hanging gold earrings, and a general air of being fairly well-to-do, in a vulgar, comfortable, easygoing way."

Sherlock Holmes clapped his hands softly together and chuckled.

"'Pon my word, Watson, you are coming along wonderfully. You have really done very well indeed. It is true that you have missed everything of importance, but you have hit upon the method, and you have a quick eye for color. Never trust to general impressions, my boy, but concentrate yourself upon details. My first glance is always at a woman's sleeve. In a man it is perhaps better first to take the knee of the trouser. As you observe, this woman had plush upon her sleeve, which is a most useful material for showing traces. The double line a little above the wrist, where the typewritist presses against the table, was beautifully defined. The sewing machine, of the hand type, leaves a similar mark, but only on the left arm, and on the side of it farthest from the thumb, instead of being right across the broadest part, as this was. I then glanced at her face, and observing the dint of a pince-nez at either side of her nose, I ventured a remark upon short sight and typewriting, which seemed to surprise her."

"It surprised me."

"But, surely, it was very obvious. I was then much surprised and interested on glancing down to observe that, though the boots which she was wearing were not unlike each other, they were really odd ones, the one having a slightly decorated toe cap and the other a plain one. One was buttoned only in the two lower buttons out of five, and the other at the first, third, and fifth. Now, when you see that a young lady, otherwise neatly dressed, has come away from home with odd boots, half-buttoned, it is no great deduction to say that she came away in a hurry."

"And what else?" I asked, keenly interested, as I always was, by my friend's incisive reasoning.

"I noted, in passing, that she had written a note before leaving home, but after being fully dressed. You observed that her right glove was torn at the forefinger, but you did not, apparently, see that both glove and finger were stained with violet ink. She had written in a hurry, and dipped her pen too deep. It must have been this morning, or the mark would not remain clear upon the finger. All this is amusing, though rather elementary, but I must go back to business, Watson. Would you mind reading me the advertised description of Mr. Hosmer Angel?"

I held the little printed slip to the light. "Missing," it said, "on the morning of the fourteenth, a gentleman named Hosmer Angel. About five feet seven inches in height; strongly built, sallow complexion, black hair, a little bald in the center, bushy black side-whiskers and mustache; tinted glasses; slight infirmity of speech. Was dressed, when last seen, in black frock-coat faced with silk, black waistcoat, gold Albert chain, and gray Harris tweed trousers, with brown gaiters over elastic-sided boots. Known to have been employed in an office in Leadenhall Street. Anybody bringing," etc., etc.

"That will do," said Holmes. "As to the letters," he continued, glancing over them, "they are very commonplace. Absolutely no clew in them to Mr. Angel, save that he quotes Balzac once. There is one remarkable point, however, which will no doubt strike you."

"They are typewritten," I remarked.

"Not only that, but the signature is typewritten. Look at the neat little 'Hosmer Angel' at the bottom. There is a date, you see, but no superscription except Leadenhall Street, which is rather vague. The point about the signature is very suggestive - in fact, we may call it conclusive."

"Of what?"

"My dear fellow, is it possible you do not see how strongly it bears upon the case?"

"I cannot say that I do, unless it were that he wished to be able to deny his signature if an action for breach of promise were instituted."

"No, that was not the point. However, I shall write two letters which should settle the matter. One is to a firm in the City, the other is to the young lady's stepfather, Mr. Windibank, asking him whether he could meet us here at six o'clock to-morrow evening. It is just as well that we should do business with the male relatives. And now, doctor, we can do nothing until the answers to those letters come, so we may put our little problem upon the shelf for the interim."

I had had so many reasons to believe in my friend's subtle powers of reasoning, and extraordinary energy in action, that I felt that he must have some solid grounds for the assured and easy demeanor with which he treated the singular mystery which he had been called upon to fathom. Once only had I known him to fail, in the case of the King of Bohemia and the Irene Adler photograph, but when I looked back to the weird business of the "Sign of the Four," and the extraordinary circumstances connected with the "Study in Scarlet," I felt that it would be a strange tangle indeed which he could not unravel.

I left him then, still puffing at his black clay pipe, with the conviction that when I came again on the next evening I would find that he held in his hands all the clews which would lead up to the identity of the disappearing bridegroom of Miss Mary Sutherland.

A professional case of great gravity was engaging my own attention at the time, and the whole of next day I was busy at the bedside of the sufferer. It was not until close upon six o'clock that I found myself free, and was able to spring into a hansom and drive to Baker Street, half afraid that I might be too late to assist at the denouement of the little mystery. I found Sherlock Holmes alone, however, half asleep, with his long, thin form curled up in the recesses of his armchair. A formidable array of bottles and test-tubes, with the pungent, cleanly smell of hydrochloric acid, told me that he had spent his day in the chemical work which was so dear to him.

"Well, have you solved it?" I asked as I entered.

"Yes. It was the bisulphate of baryta."

"No, no; the mystery!" I cried.

"Oh, that! I thought of the salt that I have been working upon. There was never any mystery in the matter, though, as I said yesterday, some of the details are of interest. The only drawback is that there is no law, I fear, that can touch the scoundrel."

"Who was he, then, and what was his object in deserting Miss Sutherland?"

The question was hardly out of my mouth, and Holmes had not yet opened his lips to reply, when we heard a heavy footfall in the passage, and a tap at the door.

"This is the girl's stepfather, Mr. James Windibank," said Holmes. "He has written to me to say that he would be here at six. Come in!"

The man who entered was a sturdy, middle-sized fellow, some thirty years of age, clean shaven, and sallow-skinned, with a bland, insinuating manner, and a pair of wonderfully sharp and penetrating gray eyes. He shot a questioning glance at each of us, placed his shiny top hat upon the sideboard, and, with a slight bow, sidled down into the nearest chair.

"Good evening, Mr. James Windibank," said Holmes. "I think this typewritten letter is from you, in which you made an appointment with me for six o'clock?"

"Yes, sir. I am afraid that I am a little late, but I am not quite my own master, you know. I am sorry that Miss Sutherland has troubled you about this little matter, for I think it is far better not to wash linen of the sort in public. It was quite against my wishes that she came, but she is a very excitable, impulsive girl, as you may have noticed, and she is not easily controlled when she has made up her mind on a point. Of course, I did not mind you so much, as you are not connected with the official police, but it is not pleasant to have a family misfortune like this noised abroad. Besides, it is a useless expense, for how could you possibly find this Hosmer Angel?"

"On the contrary," said Holmes, quietly, "I have every reason to believe that I will succeed in discovering Mr. Hosmer Angel."

Mr. Windibank gave a violent start, and dropped his gloves. "I am delighted to hear it," he said.

"It is a curious thing," remarked Holmes, "that a typewriter has really quite as much individuality as a man's handwriting. Unless they are quite new no two of them write exactly alike. Some letters get more worn than others, and some wear only on one side. Now, you remark in this note of yours, Mr. Windibank, that in every case there is some little slurring over the e, and a slight defect in the tail of the r. There are fourteen other characteristics, but those are the more obvious."

"We do all our correspondence with this machine at the office, and no doubt it is a little worn," our visitor answered, glancing keenly at Holmes with his bright little eyes.

"And now I will show you what is really a very interesting study, Mr. Windibank," Holmes continued. "I think of writing another little monograph some of these days on the typewriter and its relation to crime. It is a subject to which I have devoted some little attention. I have here four letters which purport to come from the missing man. They are all typewritten. In each case, not only are the e's slurred and the r's tailless, but you will observe, if you care to use my magnifying lens, that the fourteen other characteristics to which I have alluded are there as well."

Mr. Windibank sprung out of his chair, and picked up his hat. "I cannot waste time over this sort of fantastic talk, Mr. Holmes," he said. "If you can catch the man, catch him, and let me know when you have done it."

"Certainly," said Holmes, stepping over and turning the key in the door. "I let you know, then, that I have caught him!"

"What! where?" shouted Mr. Windibank, turning white to his lips, and glancing about him like a rat in a trap.

"Oh, it won't do - really it won't," said Holmes, suavely. "There is no possible getting out of it, Mr. Windibank. It is quite too transparent, and it was a very bad compliment when you said that it was impossible for me to solve so simple a question. That's right! Sit down, and let us talk it over."

Our visitor collapsed into a chair, with a ghastly face, and a glitter of moisture on his brow. "It - it's not actionable," he stammered.

"I am very much afraid that it is not; but between ourselves, Windibank, it was as cruel, and selfish, and heartless a trick in a petty way as ever came before me. Now, let me just run over the course of events, and you will contradict me if I go wrong."

The man sat huddled up in his chair, with his head sunk upon his breast, like one who is utterly crushed. Holmes stuck his feet up on the corner of the mantelpiece, and, leaning back with his hands in his pockets, began talking, rather to himself, as it seemed, than to us.

"The man married a woman very much older than himself for her money," said he, "and he enjoyed the use of the money of the daughter as long as she lived with them. It was a considerable sum, for people in their position, and the loss of it would have made a serious difference. It was worth an effort to preserve it. The daughter was of a good, amiable disposition, but affectionate and warmhearted in her ways, so that it was evident that with her fair personal advantages, and her little income, she would not be allowed to remain single long. Now her marriage would mean, of course, the loss of a hundred a year, so what does her stepfather do to prevent it? He takes the obvious course of keeping her at home, and forbidding her to seek the company of people of her own age. But soon he found that that would not answer forever. She became restive, insisted upon her rights, and finally announced her positive intention of going to a certain ball. What does her clever stepfather do then? He conceives an idea more creditable to his head than to his heart. With the connivance and assistance of his wife, he disguised himself, covered those keen eyes with tinted glasses, masked the face with a mustache and a pair of bushy whiskers, sunk that clear voice into an insinuating whisper, and doubly secure on account of the girl's short sight, he appears as Mr. Hosmer Angel, and keeps off other lovers by making love himself."

"It was only a joke at first," groaned our visitor. "We never thought that she would have been so carried away."

"Very likely not. However that may be, the young lady was very decidedly carried away, and having quite made up her mind that her stepfather was in France, the suspicion of treachery never for an instant entered her mind. She was flattered by the gentleman's attentions, and the effect was increased by the loudly expressed admiration of her mother. Then Mr. Angel began to call, for it was obvious that the matter should be pushed as far as if would go, if a real effect were to be produced. There were meetings, and an engagement, which would finally secure the girl's affections from turning toward anyone else. But the deception could not be kept up forever. These pretended journeys to France were rather cumbrous.

The thing to do was clearly to bring the business to an end in such a dramatic manner that it would leave a permanent impression upon the young lady's mind, and prevent her from looking upon any other suitor for some time to come. Hence those vows of fidelity exacted upon a Testament, and hence also the allusions to a possibility of something happening on the very morning of the wedding. James Windibank wished Miss Sutherland to be so bound to Hosmer Angel, and so uncertain as to his fate, that for ten years to come, at any rate, she would not listen to another man. As far as the church door he brought her, and then, as he could go no farther, he conveniently vanished away by the old trick of stepping in at one door of a four-wheeler and out at the other. I think that that was the chain of events, Mr. Windibank!"

Our visitor had recovered something of his assurance while Holmes had been talking, and he rose from his chair now with a cold sneer upon his pale face.

"It may be so, or it may not, Mr. Holmes," said he; "but if you are so very sharp you ought to be sharp enough to know that it is you who are breaking the law now, and not me. I have done nothing actionable from the first, but as long as you keep that door locked you lay yourself open to an action for assault and illegal constraint."

"The law cannot, as you say, touch you," said Holmes, unlocking and throwing open the door, "yet there never was a man who deserved punishment more. If the young lady has a brother or a friend, he ought to lay a whip across your shoulders. By Jove!" he continued, flushing up at the sight of the bitter sneer upon the man's face, "it is not part of my duties to my client, but here's a hunting crop handy, and I think I shall just treat myself to--" He took two swift steps to the whip, but before he could grasp it there was a wild clatter of steps upon the stairs, the heavy hall door banged, and from the window we could see Mr. James Windibank running at the top of his speed down the road.

"There's a cold-blooded scoundrel!" said Holmes, laughing as he threw himself down into his chair once more. "That fellow will rise from crime to crime until he does something very bad and ends on a gallows. The case has, in some respects, been not entirely devoid of interest."

"I cannot now entirely see all the steps of your reasoning," I remarked.

"Well, of course it was obvious from the first that this Mr. Hosmer Angel must have some strong object for his curious conduct, and it was equally clear that the only man who really profited by the incident, as far as we could see, was the stepfather. Then the fact that the two men were never together, but that the one always appeared when the other was away, was suggestive. So were the tinted spectacles and the curious voice, which both hinted at a disguise, as did the bushy whiskers. My suspicions were all confirmed by his peculiar action in typewriting his signature, which, of course, inferred that his handwriting was so familiar to her that she would recognize even the smallest sample of it. You see all these isolated facts, together with many minor ones, all pointed in the same direction."

"And how did you verify them?"

"Having once spotted my man, it was easy to get corroboration. I knew the firm for which this man worked. Having taken the printed description, I eliminated everything from it which could be the result of a disguise - the whiskers, the glasses, the voice - and I sent it to the firm with a request that they would inform me whether it answered to the description of any of their travelers. I had already noticed the peculiarities of the typewriter, and I wrote to the man himself at his business address, asking him if he would come here. As I expected, his reply was typewritten, and revealed the same trivial but characteristic defects. The same post brought me a letter from

Westhouse and Marbank, of Fenchurch Street, to say that the description tallied in every respect with that of their employee, James Windibank. Voila tout!"

"And Miss Sutherland?"

"If I tell her she will not believe me. You may remember the old Persian saying, 'There is danger for him who taketh the tiger cub, and danger also for whoso snatcheth a delusion from a woman.' There is as much sense in Hafiz as in Horace, and as much knowledge of the world."

ABOUT THE AUTHOR

Once upon a time Craig Stephen Copland was an English major and studied under both Northrop Frye and Marshall McLuhan at the University of Toronto way back in the 1960's. He never got over his spiritual attraction to great literature and captivating stories. Somewhere in the decades since he became a Sherlockian. He is a recent member of the Bootmakers of Toronto (www.torontobootmakers.com), and mildly addicted to the sacred canon. In real life he writes about and serves as a consultant for political campaigns in Canada and the USA (www.ConservativeGrowth.net), but would abandon that pursuit if he could possibly earn a decent living writing about Sherlock Holmes.

OTHER NEW SHERLOCK HOLMES MYSTERIES

BY CRAIG STEPHEN COPLAND

(all available immediately from Amazon)

Studying Scarlet

Starlet O'Halloran has come to London looking for her wayward husband, Brett Steward. She seeks help from Sherlock Holmes. He refuses the case until he learns that three men have already been murdered who were connected to Starlet and Brett. Then this unlikely crew of Southerners and Londoners, and a couple of unexpected new characters, must work together to save the King and the Empire. Fans of both Sherlock Holmes and *Gone with the Wind* will enjoy this parody. It is the first in the series of New Sherlock Holmes Mysteries by Craig Stephen Copland.

A Scandal in Fordlandia.

As a devoted Sherlockian you will most certainly be familiar with the wonderful story *A Scandal in Bohemia.* History now repeats itself and Holmes and Watson find themselves in Toronto in 2014. Their client is a modern version of the King of Bohemia. Yet again they must use courage and ingenuity in order to save civilization, and the Mayor, from political disaster. If you love Sherlock Holmes, you will enjoy this parody of his adventure.

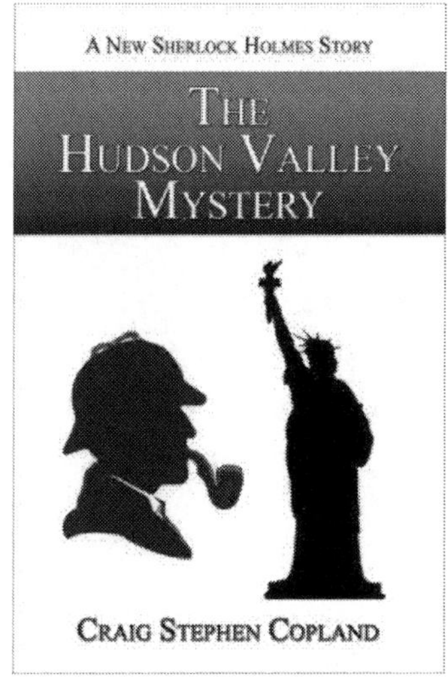

The Hudson Valley Mystery

A terrible tragedy has taken place just outside New York City. A young man murdered his father and then went stark raving mad. Sherlock Holmes is called upon by the lad's mother to solve the crime. So Sherlock Holmes and Dr. Watson make their way to America. There they meet the villains of Tammany Hall and maybe – no one will ever know – a ghostly apparition that haunts the pleasant glade known as Sleepy Hollow. The story is inspired by *The Buscombe Valley Mystery*, one of the original stories in the canon of Sherlock Holmes. The unique characters of those stories are all still present. The events and the setting may be new, but Sherlockians everywhere will recognize the mind and actions of the world's most beloved detective.

The Sign of the Third

Fifteen hundred years ago the courageous Princess Hemamali smuggled the sacred tooth of the Buddha into Ceylon. Since that time it has never left the Temple of the Tooth in Kandy, where it has been guarded and worshiped by the faithful. Now, for the first time, it is being brought to London to be part of a magnificent exhibit at the British Museum. But what if something were to happen to it? It would be a disaster for the British Empire. Sherlock Holmes, Dr. Watson and even Mycroft Holmes are called upon to prevent such a crisis. Will they prevail? What is about to happen to Dr. John Watson? And who is this mysterious young Irregular they call The Injin? This novella is inspired by the Sherlock Holmes mystery, *The Sign of the Four*. The same characters and villains are present, and fans of Arthur Conan Doyle's Sherlock Holmes will enjoy seeing their hero called upon yet again to use his powers of scientific deduction to thwart dangerous and dastardly criminals. The text of the original story is included. Your enjoyment of the book will be enhanced by re-reading the Sherlock Holmes classic and then seeing what new adventures are in store.

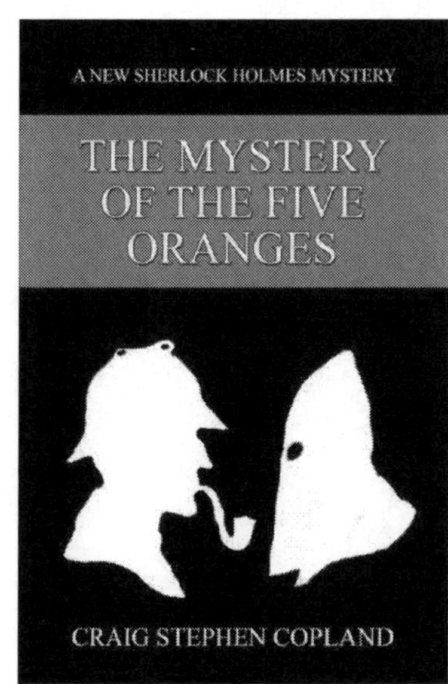

The Mystery of the Five Oranges

On a miserable rainy evening a desperate father enters 221B Baker Street. His daughter has been kidnapped and spirited off the North America. The evil network who have taken her have spies everywhere. If he goes to Scotland Yard they will kill her. There is only one hope – Sherlock Holmes.

Holmes and Watson sail to a small corner of Canada, Prince Edward Island, in search of the girl. They find themselves fighting one of the most powerful and malicious organizations on earth – the Ku Klux Klan. But they are aided in their quest by the newest member of the Baker Street Irregulars, a determined and imaginative young redhead, and by the resources of the Royal Canadian Mounted Police.

Sherlockians will enjoy this new adventure of the world's most famous detective, inspired by the original story of *The Five Orange Pips.* And those who love *Anne of Green Gables* will thrill to see her recruited by Holmes and Watson to help in the defeat of crime.

The Bald-Headed Trust

Dr. Watson insists on taking his friend on a short vacation to the seaside in Plymouth. Watson hopes that it will be a time for restoration of body and soul. Within hours of arriving there Sherlock Holmes is called upon to help solve a recent murder of two electrical engineers. What began as a tedious journey quickly turns into a puzzling and finally a diabolical adventure, as the great detective, aided by some unusual recruits to the Company of Irregulars – from the Plymouth Brethren of all people – must match wits first with bank robbers and eventually with the evil professor himself. Lovers of Sherlock Holmes mysteries will enjoy this new story, written today but as faithful as possible to the characters, heroes, villains, language, and settings of the original Sherlock Holmes.

Made in the USA
Middletown, DE
19 April 2015